SESSION

SAVING ABBIE BOOK 3

MAGGIE ALABASTER

Cover by Book Brander

Edited by Lily Luchesi

Proofread by Nora Hogan

Holding On
  Written by Tully Cole

And any way you spin the words,
  You can't help hearing yes.
  But there is never long enough,
  To tell me all the rest.

I'm holding on,
  Barely holding on.
  Saving time, for you.
  I'm holding on,
  Hardly holding on,
  To the one I never knew.

Time is an illusion,
  You know it never ends.
  But the start is no beginning,
  The healing never mends.

I'm holding on,
  Barely holding on.
  Saving time, for you.
  I'm holding on,
  Hardly holding on,
  To the one I never knew.

The choices you told me,
    The race to the lie,
    It will never be over,
    For you and him and I.

I'm holding on,
    Barely holding on.
    Saving time, for you.
    I'm holding on,
    Hardly holding on,
    To the one I'll never know.

ABBIE

"On the up side, she's quiet this way," Asher remarked. "She can't ask any stupid questions."

"Yeah, that's the takeaway here," I said.

The band and I were sitting in a hotel room in Adelaide, nearly at the end of the Australian leg of the tour, looking at the disembodied head of tabloid journalist Poppy Newton. The last time I saw her, she managed to get backstage at the festival in far North Queensland, just after I got hit in the face with a can. The band's manager, Jackson Beckett, and the owner of the label, Levi Jones, had security remove her.

Things got a little heated, but not so out of hand that I expected to see her like this.

Asher shrugged. "I'm not wrong."

"Can we stop Asher from making stupid comments?" Penn asked from where he stood near the window.

I didn't know if he was standing guard or trying to keep apart from the rest of us. Maybe both. Of all the guys, he was by far the touchiest.

I ignored Penn's comment and looked over at Zeke. "Please tell me you know a guy."

His family was basically Australian mafia. If anyone could clean up this shit, it would be them. Same with Asher's family.

Zeke shook his head slowly. "Not in this city, no," he said regretfully. "We'll figure something out."

A knock at the door made me jump so hard I wouldn't have been surprised if I hit my head on the roof.

"Jesus fucking Christ," I said under my breath.

"Landon, see who it is," Zeke said to the rhythm guitarist.

The younger guy nodded and bent to look through the peephole. "It's Jackson."

Zeke only hesitated for a moment. "Let him in. He should know about this."

Landon unlocked the door and eased it open.

Jackson looked at him funny. "Anyone would

think you guys are up to something." He stepped inside.

Landon closed and locked the door behind him. "When have we ever done anything wrong?" he asked sweetly.

Jackson raised his eyebrows at him. "Now I know you're up to something. What is it?"

"This," said Tully, the lead guitarist. He waved towards the suitcase with Poppy's head inside it.

Jackson stepped over and peered inside. His brow creased heavily. "Fuck." His face paled, then he looked a little green.

Hands to either side, he took a few steps back. "Where the hell—" He shook his head, turned and staggered into the small bathroom. He thudded to his knees in front of the toilet, retched a couple of times before being loudly, violently sick.

"I guess we can rule out his involvement," Asher said lightly.

"I'll make sure he's okay." Channing slipped into the bathroom.

"What are we going to do with her?" I perched on the edge of a chair to the side of the room. "People are going to notice her disappearance. It's been almost twenty-four hours already, if I had to guess. I mean, that's about how long it's been since I saw her."

"Same here." Jackson emerged from the bathroom, his face wet where he must have rinsed it. Channing had a hand on his shoulder. "As far as I know, security escorted her out, and she left the festival. I have no idea where she went after that."

Jackson rubbed a hand over his damp forehead. "If I knew she was going to end up like this, I would have kept tabs on her."

"Did anyone see her after she was kicked out?" Zeke asked.

"You guys were on stage at the time," I pointed out. "She was long gone before you were finished."

"That's right," Jackson said. He looked thoughtful, his eyes everywhere but on the head. "Asher, if we can repackage her and I can get a courier to take her to Melbourne, can you have your sister Rose deal with her?"

"Absolutely," Asher agreed. "I'll talk to her now. How do you guys feel about the last person she spoke to being the guy who threw the can at Abbie?"

I touched the mark on the side of my face left by the can. It could have been worse, but that asshole triggered a bunch of other people to throw cans and bottles onto the stage too. Monkey see, monkey fucking do.

In spite of that, I said, "I don't want anyone to get in trouble for a murder they didn't commit." In particular, I didn't want *us* to get blamed for a murder *we* didn't commit.

Jackson shook his head. "It wouldn't have worked. Security showed him out, but the police dealt with him shortly after. It's unlikely he would have had the chance to kill Poppy. It would be better if Rose can make it look like a nasty accident. That way, we won't have to answer any questions."

"One nasty accident on a lonely highway from far North Queensland to Sydney, coming up," Asher said cheerfully. He stepped away and started to tap at the screen on his phone.

Jackson sat on the chair beside me and cradled his face in his hands. "You realise this shit is above my pay grade, right? The average band manager doesn't deal with dead bodies. As far as I'm aware, anyway."

"You never know," Tully said. "Just because we don't hear about it doesn't mean it doesn't happen."

Jackson cocked his head at him, then shook it. "I hope it doesn't. This is all sorts of fucked up. Do we have any real idea who is doing this?"

"None," Zeke said simply. "No one's seen any of these special deliveries. They turn up when none of us are around." He looked very much like he took that personally for some reason. "It's possible one of the tour staff left this without knowing what was inside."

Jackson grimaced, but nodded. "I'll ask around, but everyone's so busy, and there's a shit ton of luggage to account for."

"And they aren't going to admit to being responsible if they are," Asher pointed out.

"That too," Jackson agreed.

"I wish they would stop," I groaned. "What's next? They kill one of you guys? If this is about me, maybe I need to drop out of the tour." How could I even consider continuing if there was a chance it will put their lives at risk? If any one of them even got a bruise because of the killer, I'd never forgive myself.

Penn opened his mouth, but closed it at a sharp look from Zeke.

"It might not be about you," Jackson said.

I did a double-take and looked at him in confusion. "What do you mean?"

"Jonah's killing might have been an attempt to get to Zeke," Jackson reasoned.

"Vance pissed off Levi because of what he did to

you. So did Calista. And Poppy, for that matter. Whoever is doing this might be targeting the label in general, trying to discredit us. You might just be collateral damage in a war that has nothing to do with you. So no, you don't get off the tour that easily." He managed a half smile.

I looked from him to Zeke. "Are you sure Reuben isn't behind all of this? Maybe he had Jonah killed to throw us off the scent?"

Zeke's mouth twisted to the side. It took him a while to respond. When he did, it came with a half shrug. "At this point, I wouldn't rule out anything or anyone. Except myself."

"It's not Levi is it?" I asked carefully. Jackson said it himself when he said people pissed Levi off. Waving a gun and threatening the lead singer of one of his more lucrative bands would not make Jonah popular with the man.

"I've known Levi Jones for the better part of a decade," Jackson said. "He would do pretty much everything for his label and his artists, but he wouldn't kill. Besides, he was with me for most of that day and night. We had dinner together before we oversaw the packing of all the equipment."

In spite of his words, there was still a sliver of doubt in the back of my mind. Someone was doing

7

this and Levi had as good a reason as Reuben. Levi wanted to protect his label the same way Reuben wanted to destroy it, or at least force Zeke out of it.

"Any chance you and Levi are working together?" Penn asked.

My brain hadn't even reached that possibility, but as soon as he asked it, I understood why. If Jackson was Levi's alibi and Levi was involved, then so was Jackson. That was a disturbing possibility.

"No," Jackson said, immediately and firmly. "I can't handle dead animals, much less people. Also, dealing with that," he jerked his head towards the suitcase containing Poppy's head, "is going to cause a shitload of hassle. Have I ever been known to cause myself unnecessary hassle?"

"You usually leave the creation of unnecessary hassle to us," Asher said.

Jackson pointed a finger gun at him. "Exactly. I didn't do this or any of the others. I can promise you that. But I will help you to deal with it. If only because we're all fucked at this point if I don't."

"We appreciate that," I said as sincerely as I could. He was taking care of us, but covering his own ass too. That was a wise move. I was a big fan of self preservation.

"It doesn't seem like we're any closer to answers

than we were before." If anything, we had more and more questions piling up on top of each other. It wasn't the kind of pile-on I liked.

I believed Jackson when he said he wasn't involved. His reaction to seeing Poppy said it all. He was genuinely surprised and horrified. And grossed out. Honestly, I couldn't see Levi doing this either, but until I was one hundred percent sure, I'd be on guard around him.

"I'll take the suitcase and get it sorted out." Jackson looked at it in disgust.

"Maybe you should discuss a pay raise with Levi?" Asher suggested. "If this keeps going on the way it is, we all should."

"You're a multimillionaire, is that not enough for you?" Penn asked, his eyes narrowed at the drummer.

Asher shrugged. "You never know when there's a rainy day coming."

"How rainy would a day have to be before you would end up broke?" Penn scoffed.

I cleared my throat. "Shit happens." Not that I was ever a millionaire, much less a multimillionaire, but it was easier to have your life go down the toilet than some people think.

Penn, of all people, should understand that.

"Unless you're going to spend your money on solid gold toilets, or private jets with hookers on them, then I think you'll do okay," Penn said to Asher. He gave me a glance like he wasn't surprised I got myself into trouble.

I resisted the urge to flip him off and said, "I can't see Asher buying solid gold toilets."

"And he doesn't need a jet with hookers on it," Zeke said.

"I might need a jet," Asher said. "Sorry to disappoint the hookers of the world, but they will have to stay at home."

"What would you need a jet for?" Tully asked.

Asher looked at me and grinned. "Because fucking Abbie in a king-size bed would be more comfortable than the plane toilet."

While I blushed, Jackson looked from him to me and back again. "Please tell me you didn't," he groaned.

I looked towards the ceiling. "Ummm."

"Me too," Zeke said smugly.

"This brings me right back to the way you guys make more hassle for me," Jackson said.

"I'm sorry?" I ventured. We couldn't go back and undo it now even if we wanted to. Which, honestly, I didn't. We didn't do anything wrong. I was over being made to feel like having emotions, and acting on them, was a bad thing.

"Yeah, well, we'll worry about that if it goes viral," Jackson said. "I would rather deal with that than this. On a scale of one to a hundred, scandals are a lot easier to deal with than murder."

"You have a lot of experience dealing with murder?" Asher asked teasingly.

Jackson fixed him with a look. "Not yet."

Asher frowned. "Hey. Are you threatening me?" He obviously knew Jackson didn't mean anything serious by it.

The guys all knew each other well enough to joke around and not to take each other too seriously. It was refreshing after the way my last label was.

Onyx Riot Records was a hot mess at best. Not just when it came to me. Everyone there was in it for themselves. They would climb over each other to succeed.

Vance, my husband for twenty-six hours, was a good example of exactly that. I thought he cared about me until after we got married and he admitted he'd done it for publicity.

I should have seen it coming, but love is too fucking blind sometimes.

"I don't threaten," Jackson said lightly. "I promise."

A smile tugged at the corners of his mouth. He would no more hurt Asher than I would. Unless that was what Asher was into.

"Now, don't make me threaten you with what might happen if you're late for tonight's concert." He got to his feet and waited for Zeke to zip the suitcase before he gripped the handle and rolled it towards the door.

"Will it be a public whipping?" Asher asked.

"Don't threaten us with a good time," Tully said with a grin.

Jackson snorted before he let himself out of the hotel room.

2

TULLY

I WATCHED Abbie's face while all of this went down. One minute, we were having a nice afternoon, and the next everything went to shit.

Again.

While part of me wished I was responsible for—how do I put this—delivering the heads of her enemies to her door, literally, I hated seeing what this was doing to her. She'd been through enough rough shit in the last year or so without body parts turning up unexpectedly.

Okay, if they turned up expectedly, that would also be bad.

I believed Jackson when he said he hadn't done it. I've known him for long enough to know he's like a protective bulldog when it came to his acts, but not a murderer.

Out of him and Levi, Levi made more sense. Even then, I didn't see it.

Zeke's family made more sense. Or Asher's. Reluctantly, I added mine to the list.

I told Abbie I had an ordinary upbringing. Some day I'd have to tell her the rest. If—when—I got past my fears about how she'd react. I owed her the whole truth. She needed to know before things went deeper between us. Would she still want to, if she knew? Like so many things lately, I had no answers for that either.

"We should try to eat something and get ready for tonight's concert," Zeke said reluctantly.

I couldn't even tell you when he started to be the leader of the group, as well as the lead singer of the band, but none of us questioned it. We didn't always do what he told us to, but we usually followed along. It was easier than arguing, and he was often right. Just don't tell him that. His ego is big enough.

I lowered myself in the chair beside Abbie, took her hand and gently pulled her onto my lap. She looked surprised but didn't protest. Instead, she nestled into me and let me tuck my arms around her.

I liked holding her like this. I felt as if I'd waited

forever to be with her the way Asher and Zeke had, but I needed to wait a bit longer. Until our date in Perth. Then I would introduce her to all the things I liked and let her explore and find what she liked.

Until then, I'd rely on my imagination. That went to some wild places I hoped she'd go for real. In particular, the thought of her blindfolded and tethered to a bed made my heart race and my cock get a little harder.

Judging by the flicker of her eyelids, she felt it poke into her thigh. She smiled and wriggled her ass a little bit.

"If you keep doing that, we're going to miss the concert," I whispered in her ear.

"The audience might not notice if I'm not there," she said bitterly. "But I'm pretty sure they'll notice if you aren't."

"They *will* notice if you miss it," I said. "You're right though. The absence of the lead guitarist would cause a stir." Shame, I could think of a few fun things we could do instead of getting up on stage and performing.

"We could always ask Blaise to play with us," Zeke offered, a trace of a sly smile on his lips.

Smart ass.

I rolled my eyes at him. "As good as Blaise is, I don't think he knows our songs as well as I do."

The lead guitarist of Blazing Violet, our support act, was amazing. I'd love the opportunity to play with him sometime, but I wasn't ready to have him replace me quite yet.

"Which is Tully's way of saying fuck off," Asher said.

"I knew that." Zeke nodded.

"Hey, I'm also capable of telling Zeke to fuck off," I said to Asher. I looked straight at Zeke and said, "Fuck off."

Zeke chuckled. "Right back at you, dude." He grabbed his phone. "What does everyone feel like?"

I wanted to taste Abbie's pussy, but instead I said, "I could go for a burger."

"Burger sounds good," Penn said.

"Something vegetarian," Abbie said. "I've seen enough meat for one day."

Zeke and Asher grinned.

I chuckled.

Penn rolled his eyes.

"I was talking about the human head," Abbie said, looking slightly sick. "The kind that goes on shoulders. I never get tired of seeing the other kind."

"That's good," Zeke said. "For a minute there I thought I traumatised you with my cock."

"If anyone's cock would traumatise you, it would be Zeke's," Penn said.

"That's because it's so big it's shocking," Zeke said.

Penn snorted. "You wish."

"We could spend the rest of the afternoon talking about Zeke's cock, or we could get some food," Landon said.

"Or we could do both," Channing suggested.

The pair never made any secret of their bisexuality. They had a reasonably solid relationship and only slept with women when they were both involved. Sooner or later, that would extend to Abbie. We all knew that, it was just a matter of when.

She was taking her time getting to know each of us, and we were getting to know her. As far as all of us were concerned, there was no rush.

In the meantime, there were no other women in our lives, romantically or sexually. That was another thing that just…happened, but it felt right. With her in my arms like she was right now, I didn't want to touch anyone else.

"I vote for both," Asher said.

He and Zeke had a thing the way Channing and Landon did, but theirs was new. It seemed to me they only just admitted their bisexuality to themselves. The pair had been friends since they were kids, but lovers only recently. They also put Abbie in the centre of everything they did. I wasn't sure if they had, or even would, be with each other without her present.

That was one hundred percent their decision and I respected it.

Someday, I would like to share her with them, but first I would like to have her to myself. We had a lot to explore and learn about each other. I was looking forward to every single moment of it.

"Okay burgers with meat for the guys. Burger with vegetarian shit for Abbie. Talking about my cock, optional," Zeke said. "I'll order all the side salads and crap as well."

"You make it sound so appetising," Penn said sarcastically.

Zeke didn't glance up from his screen. "You don't have to have any, Penny. You can always watch us eat."

"Fuck off," Penn told him.

"I thought you'd feel that way," Zeke said. "Okay, it should be here in about twenty minutes."

"One of the best things about going on tour is not having to cook," Asher remarked.

"Since when did you cook?" I asked him.

He shrugged. "I don't, but when I'm on tour I don't have to feel bad about it."

"I'll make a note to ask Jackson to pack a portable kitchen for you," Zeke said teasingly.

"Go for it, but I'm not gonna use it," Asher said. "A portable incinerator might come in useful."

"Is that even a thing? Landon asked.

"If it isn't, then it should be," Asher said. "It would make it much easier for people to dispose of their enemies."

"I think, on average, most people don't have enough enemies to justify buying something like that," I pointed out.

"Certainly not after buying it," Asher agreed. "You're right though. I don't have any enemies that I know of. Unless Jackson was right about the killer targeting the label in general. The enemy of my label is my enemy."

"You should get that on a T-shirt," Zeke said. "I'll take one in every colour."

"Thanks, babe." Asher gave him a quick kiss on the mouth. "You'd look cute in a purple one."

"Of course I would." Zeke pretended to fluff his hair. "I look good in everything." He grinned and kissed Asher back.

Penn snorted. "Says you."

"Says me too," Asher said.

"Me three," Abbie said. "But you all do."

"Even me?" Penn asked.

"Even you," she agreed. "You're pretty on the outside, even if you're an asshole on the inside." She said it in the same teasing banter we all used with each other.

"Funny, I was thinking the same about you," Penn retorted.

His icy attitude towards her was slowly melting. Very slowly, but it was happening. Some day he might even relax his attitude towards himself.

Yeah, that might be a bigger ask.

"At least you admit I'm pretty," Abbie said.

"I never said you weren't. Doesn't mean you're not a pain in the ass." Penn shrugged.

A couple of weeks ago, we would have rounded on him for saying things like that to her. Now, there was no real malice behind his words.

Besides, she could stick up for herself.

"According to the tracker, our food will be here in a minute," Zeke said. He didn't seem concerned that the conversation had turned away from his cock. There was always the possibility we could change back to that topic at any moment. We were nothing if not unpredictable.

"Let's wait outside for it," Landon said to Channing.

"Make sure no one else drops off a head before the food comes," Asher said.

Landon flashed him a grin. "I make no promises."

Abbie groaned. "With any luck, that will be the last one."

"Aren't you out of enemies yet?" Penn asked.

"I wouldn't have thought of any of them as enemies," she said slowly. "As far as I know, the only one left I had any trouble with, apart from you, is Pete. We've already established that you wouldn't let anyone cut off your head, so that leaves Pete."

"Should we warn him?" Asher asked.

"And say what?" Zeke asked. "He's already had his wife's disappearance pinned on him, and the police are looking into him in relation to Vance's death. We can't warn him that someone might come after him and avoid him going to the police to clear his name. It's already too fucking messy as it is."

"I suppose so." Asher shrugged. "There's no loss if he ends up dead, is there Abbie?"

Her body went stiff in my arms. "I don't want him dead, but when I said his wife wanted me kicked off the label after our fling, I might not have told you everything."

I brushed hair back off her cheek. "What is there?" I asked gently.

She sighed. "Pete comforted me after what Vance did. We only slept together a couple of times, as a spur of the moment thing when I was... At my lowest."

I instantly wanted to punch this Pete guy in the cock.

"What an asshole," Asher said. "I'm almost starting to look forward to seeing his head in a box."

Abbie wrinkled her nose. "Don't say that. He took advantage, but so did I. He was estranged from his wife, he was as vulnerable as I was. Maybe my head deserves to be in a box."

"Never," Zeke growled.

"There's more?" I pressed lightly.

She nodded. "When he and Calista got back together, he admitted what he did with me. She insisted he kick me off the label and made him choose between that and her. What choice did he have?"

"But?" I prompted. She clearly had more she wanted to share, but it hurt her to do it.

Seeing her in this kind of discomfort made my heart hurt.

She sighed and her tongue darted across her lower lip. She took another couple of moments to compose herself, or her thoughts.

"In order to terminate the contract, he used the unbecoming behaviour clause in my contract," she finished.

We all took a moment to absorb that.

"Fuck." Apparently Zeke absorbed it faster than the rest of us. "You sleeping with him was inappropriate behaviour for someone signed to his label?"

"Motherfucker." Asher looked like he was about ready to put his fist through the wall. "What a fucking hypocrite."

I held Abbie closer and stroked her hair. "That's a bullshit thing to do."

She shrugged. "He told everyone I had an affair with a co-worker, and that was it. I was gone. I thought about suing him, but after everything I'd been through... It was too much."

"Do you want me to take a hit out on him?" Zeke asked. He didn't seem to be joking.

"Tempting, but no," she said reluctantly. "It is what it is now. If he hadn't done what he did, I wouldn't have signed with White Wolf and I wouldn't have met you guys the way I did."

I smiled. It seemed she'd gotten on board with my philosophy that we were meant to be together, no matter what. I firmly believed we would have found each other somehow. If not in this life, then in the next.

"Remind me to thank him if I meet him," I said. "Before I kick his ass."

"Food is here," Landon said as he and Channing stepped back inside.

That ended the conversation, but not the anger that lingered in the back of my mind.

3

TULLY

"Hello Adelaide!" Zeke said into the microphone.

The crowd roared.

They responded enthusiastically to Blazing Violet, and to Abbie.

It was her first performance since the festival; she was anxious. We were all anxious for her. For a while there, before she went on, I thought she might turn and run away.

Fortunately, she didn't. Or unfortunately, since there was still the potential threat of a public whipping for missing the concert. Or maybe a private whipping, just for me and her.

With that thought in my mind and suddenly heavy balls, I stepped out on stage and swung the strap of my black and gold guitar over my head.

Ever since I held my first guitar at the age of eight, it felt comfortable in my hands. Like I was made for the instrument and it was made for me.

I'd like to say I was a prodigy like Penn and immediately knew how to play, but that would be a flat out lie. I had lessons from a guy down the street, who needed the money because his band hadn't taken off yet. Like anyone obsessed with playing an instrument, I practised every chance I got.

When I got my first electric guitar at age thirteen, I was up half the night practising, with headphones plugged into my amp. I don't think my parents realised how little sleep I got, but no regrets from me. I didn't fail at school, so no harm, right?

"Let me introduce us," Zeke said. *"We're Wolf Venom!"*

The crowd roared and started to chant. "Venom! Venom! Venom!"

We launched into our first song for the night, 'Holding On'. The crowd screamed so loud I didn't know if they could hear us or not.

They soon settled down and danced and sang along with us.

While I played, my gaze skimmed along the row of people who stood at the front. A lot of them had Wolf Venom T-shirts in every colour they came in.

Unfortunately, I couldn't see anyone dressed as fruit. Not even an animal costume. Maybe I should get myself a carrot costume to wear on stage. Jackson would love that.

Not.

Zeke danced past me, microphone in one hand, the other raised to encourage the audience to clap along. Many of them did, but most people had a phone in their hand, filming us.

I knew some musicians hated when audiences did that. More than one tried to ban phones from their concerts altogether. Personally, it didn't worry me. As long as people were enjoying themselves, then there was nothing wrong with having a memento to watch later. In a year or two, when they'd forgotten who we were, they'd probably delete the footage from their phones anyway.

Unless one of us did something super embarrassing, like falling over, or tumbling off the side of the stage. That shit would follow us around forever.

I turned at movement in the corner of my eye.

Abbie stepped back on stage to sing with Zeke.

Not long ago, Penn violently and loudly objected to her singing on stage with us.

Now, he looked up from his keyboard and watched her walking too. He probably thought no one was paying attention to him, but I saw the hunger in his eyes.

I didn't blame him. She was a beautiful woman with the most incredible, lush body I ever saw. She wasn't afraid of her sexuality, or the connection she was developing with all of us. Other women might run away from the prospect of becoming involved with six, somewhat crazy, guys. But not Abbie. She seemed to love every minute of it.

She pulled the other microphone out of the stand and stepped over to Zeke on her long, shapely legs. Even in heels, she was shorter than the lead singer. Than any of us. She was small but perfectly formed.

She straightened the hem of her skirt which fell halfway down her delicious thighs, and raised the microphone to her luscious lips.

"Hey," she said to Zeke as if she wasn't standing on stage in front of thousands of people.

"Hey." He turned to her. "Fancy meeting you here. Do you *come* here often?" No one in the arena missed the inflection.

The audience laughed.

"Not yet," she replied with a laugh. "I figured you could use some help on a couple of songs."

The audience cheered.

"Yeah?" Zeke asked. He turned to look at the

crowd and stretched out his hand. "I would appreciate a hand." He grinned.

The audience snickered. More than one woman shouted out her willingness to give him one. Or a mouth.

I didn't doubt they meant it too. Zeke had that impact on women. And men.

Channing played a short, seductive tune on his saxophone.

Zeke chuckled and he and Abbie started singing, 'In Deeper', which fit perfectly with the suggestive introduction. Of course, that was the point. To get the audience going before the sexy lyrics. The crowd didn't even seem to mind that Zeke and Abbie were clearly singing to each other. If I was the jealous kind, I would be envious of the obvious connection.

I wasn't though; Abbie and I had a connection of our own.

They finished their two songs and we all put down, or stepped away from, our instruments, except Penn. The rest of us hurried off stage to let him do his solo and to have a quick toilet break, and change out of our sweat-drenched tees.

Abbie and I stopped and stood at the bottom of the steps to the backstage area to listen to what song he chose that night. Every night it was different. He claimed he didn't know what song he was going to play and sing until he actually began.

I had no reason not to believe him. Sometimes all we could do was go where the music took us. And the mood of the audience. He always nailed that too, giving them what they probably didn't know they wanted.

He placed his fingers on his keyboard, leaned forward to the microphone and started to sing 'Imagine', of all things.

"How does he do that?" Abbie asked. "He can be such a dickhead, but then he plays and sings so beautifully, I want to cry."

I slipped an arm around her waist and fitted her in against my hip. "He's a complicated guy." No one would argue he was insanely talented as well. He could easily go out by himself as a solo artist. It was a good thing he didn't, since the band was better for having him as a part of it.

We were a dysfunctional family at times, okay, a lot of the time, but we had each other's backs. That was one of the reasons he stuck with us. And why we put up with him when he was being a grumpy pain in the ass.

I stood on my toes and peered up the steps towards the audience. All I could see was thousands and thousands of phone lights waving slowly back and forth, like a sky full of dancing stars.

I lowered myself back down as Jackson joined us. He placed a hand on the wall beside him and watched, a thoughtful look on his face.

"What?" I asked him.

He turned his face towards me and cocked his head. "What?"

"You look like you're thinking something," I said. "Should we be scared? Or is the public whipping coming up next?"

He rolled his eyes towards the ceiling and smiled. "No public whipping. At least not today. I think there are laws against shit like that."

"Hey, as long as everyone is consenting..." I grinned. "So what are you actually thinking? You didn't tell me if I should be scared or not."

"You shouldn't be," he said. "It doesn't involve you. And anyway, it's just a thought at the moment. I'll have to run it past Levi or one of the executives."

"Are you going to put his keyboard on a platform that lifts up off the stage?" Abbie asked.

Jackson quirked an eyebrow at her. "I wasn't going to, but that's not a bad idea. Maybe for the next tour."

"You could elevate Asher too," I said, grinning.

"They could sit up in the back and look down at us all."

"I see you like to spend the label's money," Jackson said dryly. "Too much of that would get expensive and difficult. Not to mention how much that would cost to insure. And the risk of broken bones."

In spite of his words, he didn't look as though he hated the idea. On the other hand, we were always trying to come up with ways to make each tour different and special. I had a feeling this idea wouldn't fly, so to speak, for all the reasons he mentioned. We'd have to come up with something else.

Which begged the question, what was Jackson thinking? He obviously wasn't going to tell us until he was ready, which sucked. One way or another, I'd find out.

"You're welcome," I said. We made a ton of money for the label, why shouldn't we have some say in how to spend it? Honestly, I suspected Asher would hate being elevated like that anyway. He preferred to sit back behind his drums and make an impact with his beat, not with showy theatrics.

Jackson smirked and we all turned back to listen to Penn.

Penn kept the audience captivated until the very last note died away.

Just in time, the other guys trotted back from the toilet, each dressed in clean, dry shirts.

I gave Abbie a quick kiss on the mouth, as did Asher and Zeke, then we headed back onto the stage to a rousing applause.

Zeke grabbed his microphone back out of the stand. "Beau Pennington, ladies and gentlemen." He waved towards Penn, who gave the audience a seated bow as they cheered and clapped.

"I don't know if I can follow that," Zeke told the fifty-three thousand strong crowd in confidence.

They cheered.

"Probably not," Penn said into his mic. He didn't smile but he looked smug.

It was a miracle his ego wasn't bigger than it already was. Plenty of guys as talented as him were absolute nightmares. I knew one who wouldn't even share his hotel room with anyone else in the band or on the tour. And that was before he got big enough to afford a separate room.

Penn was arrogant, but he was also realistic. Some of the time anyway.

The audience laughed.

Zeke turned and pretended to wave to someone

off stage. "Can we get his microphone turned off please?"

Again, the audience laughed, and many shouted, "No!"

Penn shrugged. "Thanks everyone. I'll send you all your fifty dollars each after the concert." He sat back and laced his hands behind his head as though he was done for the night.

It wasn't often he joked around. Abbie must have made a good impact on him if he was doing it now. By the time she was done, he might even smile once in a while.

Predictably, the audience roared louder than ever. Who wouldn't like fifty dollars just for getting behind Penn? Hell, I'd take it.

Zeke laughed and nodded. That was our cue to launch into the next song.

4

ABBIE

IT WASN'T until after the concert and before the meet and greet that I got a chance to catch up with Jackson.

"Did you deal with it?" I asked, deliberately vague in case anyone overheard.

"Yep," he said simply. "As long as Asher dealt with his side, then it's sorted."

"Do you really think it's not about me?" I asked tentatively. I wanted to believe that. I really did, but if they were going after the label, surely they would go after people like Candy, Jackson or even Levi himself? On the other hand, if they did that, the target would be obvious. Wouldn't it?

Hell, I didn't even know any more.

He rubbed his chin. It looked like he hadn't

shaved in a few days. That was understandable given how busy tours were.

"I don't know," he admitted. "Unless whomever is doing this leaves a note or is caught, we may never know the real reason. It might be over now, for all we know."

"I hope so," I said. "There's enough pressure on all of us without…that."

"You're not fucking wrong there," he said. "Just in case, keep an eye out at the meet and greet. Let me know if anyone looks familiar. I know of a few instances where enthusiastic fans turne up at these kinds of things. Often repeatedly. Sometimes they're just enthusiastic fans. Other times they're more."

"Stalkers?" I had heard of the same thing happening, but I couldn't recall seeing the same faces over and over again at past meet and greets. Was I looking? No, not really. Faces blurred together eventually.

"Possibly," he agreed. "If they have a chance to get close to the object of their obsession, they will. Meets and greets are a good way to do it. Where else but a place you can get near and blend in at the same time? It's twisted as shit but people aren't always reasonable."

I snorted. "Really? What a shocker." I patted his

shoulder. "Sorry to be sarcastic but that might be the understatement of the century."

He smiled.

He had become like a big brother to me. That was what I needed during this crazy ride. Several boyfriends and a big brother. A girl would have to be safe with all of them around, wouldn't she?

"Just slightly," he agreed. "Fortunately we're surrounded by the members of two bands who are *always* reasonable." He made a face.

I laughed. "So what were you thinking while Penn was playing?" I asked, hoping to catch him off guard. I knew Tully wanted to know, and I certainly did.

"Don't tell me they're rubbing off on you," he said with a groan. "I can't talk about it just now. When I can, you'll be one of the first to know."

"Okay, now I'm scared," I said, my eyes wide. "You're not gonna put me on a platform are you?"

He chuckled. "I would, since it was your idea in the first place, but the insurance would still be ridiculously expensive. Cables would be safer." He looked thoughtful, but he hadn't quite stopped smiling.

"The guys are rubbing off on *who* now?" I teased.

"Maybe I rubbed off on them?" he suggested.

"If that's the case, then you only have yourself to blame," I said dryly.

"Huh. In that case, they are rubbing off on me. Don't worry, it doesn't involve cables, platforms or anything particularly dangerous."

"Particularly dangerous?" I echoed. "So it's dangerous?" I wasn't sure I liked the sound of that.

"Not physically dangerous." He gave me a cagey look.

"I know it's not going to jeopardise my career," I said. "After everything that's happened, you wouldn't do that to me."

I hoped.

"Absolutely not," he said. "Exactly the opposite."

"Are you really going to get me this intrigued and then not tell me?" I complained.

He smiled. "Yes."

"That is pure evil," I told him. "I thought you were nice too."

He laughed. "I am nice. Trust me, it will be one hundred percent worth the wait."

At this point, the only thing I could think of was a plan for a solo tour. I liked that idea, but I didn't know why he wouldn't just come out and say that. Unless he had to run it past Levi first. That made sense, I suppose.

"What happens if it isn't?" I asked.

Before I could even mention it, he said, "No public whippings."

I sighed dramatically. "Oh bugger, I was looking forward to that."

"Too much information." He grimaced.

"Does that bother you that I'm in a relationship with Zeke and Asher?" I asked. "And that Tully and I are going on a date when we get to Perth?"

"And that Penn, Channing and Landon all look at you the way the other three do?" he said. "It was unexpected, but not entirely surprising. I mean, I didn't see it coming before you met the guys, but if any group of men was going to share a woman, it would be them. Okay, and the guys of Blazing Violet, with Violet, even if they don't see it yet."

"You don't think that's weird at all?" I asked.

"Should I?" he asked. "I've been around for a while and I've seen all sorts of different things and different relationships. What you're doing is, I think, more normal than other people realise."

"Would you do it?" I asked.

He looked surprised at the question, but then thoughtful. "I might if the right situation came along. I'm away so much of the time, would it be fair to ask a woman to wait at home alone? At least this way, she would always have other people around when she needed them."

I tilted my head. "That's very enlightened of you. A lot of guys would just go away and not worry about what the woman thought or felt."

He shrugged one shoulder. "It's not the seventeen hundreds anymore." He gave me a long look before adding, "Have you thought about what happens after the tour?"

I straightened my head and shook it. "I've stressed about it, but we haven't talked about it or anything. I mean, things are new. I don't want to make any assumptions about the way anyone else is feeling or what they're thinking."

"I can make a few," he said. "But I can also understand your reluctance to plan for the rest of your life right now. Especially with all the—" He cleared his throat.

"Yes, all *the*," I agreed. "It looks like the meet and greet is about to start. I don't suppose anyone is waiting to meet me." Except maybe potential stalkers. They could wait forever.

"Several," he said. "You're more popular than you think. I'll stay close by all night, until the meet and greet is over, just in case anyone tries anything funny. This is one time when the guys have to do their own thing, rather than watching over you. I don't want to give security too much information, for obvious reasons. After the can throwing incident, they know to keep an eye out for you or anyone behaving strangely. That has put everyone on edge. How are you feeling after that?" He peered at my cheek.

"I'm okay," I said lightly. "Going out on stage tonight was daunting, but once I was out there I was fine. Plus, people can't bring cans or bottles into the venue." That went a long way to settling my nerves a couple of hours ago.

"Good, I'm glad you bounced back so quickly," he said approvingly. "I know plenty of singers who would have refused to go out on another stage again after that."

"My career wouldn't last very long if I ran away every time shit like that happened," I said dryly. Fuck knows I had plenty of excuses to quit, but I hadn't taken any of them.

If anything, I was more determined. I wasn't going to let a little tin can, or aluminium can, ruin the rest of my life.

Disembodied heads, that was a different story.

"That's why the most successful people are the ones who have stuck it out," he said. "The guys have had plenty of chances and reasons for quitting, but they haven't. Actually, I'm not sure they would let each other quit."

"Yeah, they would give each other hell if anyone suggested it," I agreed. "They're a pretty amazing team."

"They are," he agreed. "And you are a pretty amazing addition to it. Levi knew what he was doing. Obviously. He's gotten rich knowing what he was doing."

I blushed at his words. "I'm not sure Levi knew entirely what he was doing. I mean, he wouldn't have guessed I might end up in a relationship with the guys."

Jackson leaned his shoulder against the wall and crossed his arms over his chest. "I wouldn't underestimate what Levi Jones would or wouldn't have guessed. He knows all of the guys pretty well. I wouldn't be surprised if he has a bet with someone that you would get together with at least one of the guys."

I matched his pose by crossing my arms. "Have you got a bet with him?"

He smiled slightly. "I might. I might not. It wouldn't be professional of me if I did, would it? It certainly wouldn't be professional of me to admit it."

I surprise myself by feeling comfortable enough with him to poke my finger into his chest. "You really are as bad as the guys, aren't you?"

He grinned. "There's a reason Levi chose me as their manager and not someone else. Who else would put up with them but someone as batshit crazy as they are?"

"I think you just called me crazy, in a roundabout way," I said slowly. I squinted at him. "But I'm not sure."

"I think I'll leave it up to you to interpret it however you want." He straightened up. "Okay, security is letting people in. Remember, I won't be far away. I'll be watching the whole time."

I nodded. Nerves that hadn't been there a moment ago fluttered through my belly.

"I appreciate it." I meant that. It was good to have someone looking out for me when the guys were busy with their fans. I trusted Jackson as much as I trusted any of them. Maybe more so, because I wasn't clouded with lust when it came to him. I liked him, but I would never look at him that way.

Would I?

I stood awkwardly while security herded people in my direction. The smiles on their faces were gratifying. After the festival and not just the cans but also the words, it was nice to be greeted by people who were actually happy to see me.

"Hey," I greeted the first in line, two women about the same age as me. They both looked about ready to jump up and down with excitement.

"Oh my God, I can't believe we get to meet you," the taller one with short, dark hair gushed.

"I keep thinking we're dreaming," the shorter one, with long blond hair, agreed. Her blue eyes were huge with genuine joy.

Meeting people like this made doing my job more worthwhile than anything else. It made me realise I was actually touching people by just opening my mouth and singing.

What could be more rewarding than that?

"If you're dreaming, than I am too," I said. "Should I pinch myself and see if we wake up?"

"No!" The brunette waved her hand at me. "I don't want to wake up. Can we get a selfie?"

"Of course." While I got into place beside them, I scanned the line of people waiting to meet me. No one looked familiar, strange, or out of place, but I wouldn't relax fully until this was over. After all, what did a stalker look like anyway? Probably just a regular person. One you would never suspect of stalking and killing people.

I smiled when both women held up their phones and took photos. I didn't stop smiling for another hour or two after that.

My face was going to hurt tomorrow, but I loved every minute of it.

5

ABBIE

"I ALWAYS FORGET how pretty Perth is." I looked out at the Swan River, which meandered past the restaurant. "This is nice."

"It is nice," Tully agreed. "It's nice to have you to myself. The other guys are adorable and all that shit, but I've been looking forward to having time alone."

"Me too." I turned to give him a soft smile. "I keep thinking I'm going to look over my shoulder and see the rest of the guys watching over us or something."

"I do too," he admitted. "They're probably hiding out somewhere we can't see them." He pointed at a building across the river. "Like in there, with binoculars on us. Just in case—" He flipped off the building.

I laughed. "Would they be that far away? They're more likely to be hiding behind a bush or around a corner." I waved in no particular direction. "Except Penn. I can't imagine him bothering to hide."

"He's probably in the hotel bar, drinking," Tully agreed. "That's more his speed."

"That sounds accurate," I said. That was where they all were when we left. According to Asher, they were going to have a couple of drinks and then head to dinner.

"Can I ask you a question?" I slowly turned my wineglass around, my fingers on the stem.

"Of course," he said without hesitation.

"Just like that?" I asked. "What if I ask you something you don't want to answer?"

He took a sip of his beer. "Then I'll tell you I won't answer it. But most things are an open book as far as I'm concerned."

"Now I'm thinking I should ask you something more personal," I said. "I was just going to ask about groupies. I've seen a few hanging around since we arrived."

"Yeah." He put down his beer and picked up his fork. "Is this where you ask what the other guys might get up to when you're not looking? Are you worried they're all hooking up with different people as we speak?"

"I probably sound paranoid." I grimaced.

"They've given me no reason to think they would, especially Zeke and Asher, but they are rock gods. If you guys share me, what right do I have to expect them not to do what they want, with whoever they want?"

I hated the idea of sharing them with anyone apart from each other, but here I was, sitting with Tully. Was I a hypocrite?

"This might come as a shock, especially coming from a guy," he said slowly, "but there's more to life than sex. We all care about you, a lot, and none of us want to lose you. This arrangement, this sharing thing, is something new and different for us. But..." He wrinkled his brow in thought.

"We each give each other different things," he said finally. "We're friends as well as bandmates. We're brothers, if you like. We play together and we don't go and play with other bands, generally speaking. You give each of us something different too. Like Zeke and Asher give each other something different. Like Landon and Channing do." He paused for a moment.

"It's like how a song is made up of a bunch of notes. Those notes appear in a lot of different songs, but when you put them together in a certain way, they make something special and unique."

"Musical notes aren't known for being exclusive," I pointed out.

"No, but certain combinations of them are, or people get sued," Tully said. "Trust that the guys care about you enough to be a part of this song instead of running off after a new one. Speaking for myself, I haven't been interested in another tune since I met you. I feel—I don't know—whole somehow. Like we had the song but we were lacking the right tempo."

I blushed at that, but I knew what he meant. All my life I was missing something and now I knew what it was. I just didn't expect it to be six guys.

Was that greedy of me? Or was it just that when the right tune was made, all we could do was roll with it?

"Can I be the tranquillo?" I asked. I would happily set the tempo to tranquil and peaceful, rather than the wild, frenetic pace of the last year or so.

"That would suit you," he agreed. "Or maybe something a little faster. Not too fast, but fast enough that we have to work hard to keep up with you. You wouldn't want to make it too easy on us." He grinned and stabbed his fork into his ravioli.

"No, not too easy." I wound spaghetti around my fork and managed to get it into my mouth without dropping it everywhere.

Bonus.

"So you had an ordinary childhood compared to Asher and Zeke?" I asked once I swallowed.

He hesitated.

"You don't have to talk about it if you don't want to," I said quickly.

Childhoods were a touchy subject with these guys. With good reason. Zeke and Asher's family were into some bad shit and from what I knew, Penn's family had expectations of him he struggled to meet. I had no idea about any of the other guys.

"It's okay," he said slowly. "I told you I had an ordinary childhood, but that wasn't the whole story. I was taken from my family when I was about six and raised by the people I think of as my parents. My biological parents were associates of the Brantley family."

Why did that not surprise me? They seemed to have their fingers in a shitload of pies, and lives.

"I'm guessing things didn't go well?" I asked as gently as I could. "What happened?"

"My mother was the second best assassin in Melbourne," Tully said.

"Second-best?" I echoed. Wait, did he say *assassin*? Yes, he had.

Shit.

"Someone hired her to take out a hit on one of the Bell family. They took that as well as you might expect. In return, they hired the first best assassin to take her out."

"That sounds like a movie," I muttered.

He smiled and his eyebrows jerked upward quickly. "It does." He took a gulp of beer. "My father lost it after that. Started drinking, getting into all sorts of shit he shouldn't get into. He pissed off a lot of people. One night, he got into a fight he couldn't win and ended up dead on the side of the road."

"Oh God," I breathed. "That's terrible." No wonder he was reluctant to talk about it.

Tully shrugged. "No loss. He was getting violent at home. Nothing I couldn't handle, but it was getting more and more out of hand. I was going to go and live with my aunt, but Zeke's father stepped in and pulled some strings to have me placed with the family that adopted me. My aunt was almost as bad as my father."

"That's the first time I've heard of anyone with the last name Brantley, other than Zeke, doing something nice," I said.

He shrugged again. "I was the same age as Zeke. Apparently he had a soft spot for me, because of my mother. He wasn't too happy she was killed."

"I'm sure you weren't either," I said.

"No, but I hardly remember her." He took another gulp of beer. "She was often away. I had no idea why at the time. I would never have guessed if I tried. I mean, what kid guesses his mother is a hitwoman?"

"I think superhero is usually about as outrageous as it gets," I said. "Or aliens from another planet. I always hoped mine came from Saturn. Until I was about seven, I waited for a spaceship to come and collect us." I rolled my eyes at my own silly childhood fantasy.

"And then you became a singer instead," he said. "That's a childhood fantasy that doesn't come true for most people. But for you it did."

"I often wonder why," I admitted. "Why me and not a billion other talented girls? Plenty of them work as hard as I do and are just as good, if not better than me. Tons are prettier and have better bodies than I do, which shouldn't be a requirement, but it often is."

I hated that aspect of the industry. Being talented and wanting to put in the work, that should be enough.

"That's easy," Tully said. "There's something about you. Something that makes people sit up and take notice. It's not just that you're beautiful and have a smoking hot body, which you do. People want to watch you and be around you. The things that happened to you in the past, was all because other people are jealous of that magnetism you have."

"And my ability to make dumb choices," I said dryly.

He leaned forward and put his hand on mine. He looked me straight in the eyes. "People took advantage of your sweet nature, but I promise you there was a lot of jealousy involved. Vance wanted what you had. Calista too. And Poppy. If I dig down deep, I'll probably find that Poppy Newton was a frustrated singer who couldn't make it. Or an actor maybe. Something you are and she could never be."

"Possibly." I wanted to believe that. Not that people were jealous of me, but that things didn't happen because I was a complete dumbass.

"Definitely," he said firmly.

"What about Jonah then?" I asked. "Was he jealous of Zeke?"

"Probably," Tully said. "Who would want to be a street thug when you can be a rock star?"

"Reuben?" I asked.

Tully laughed. "I'd love to see you call Reuben a street thug to his face. But don't do it if you value your life. He likes to think he's a long way above all of that shit. Above street gangs and above the law. He's the king of the castle and we're the dirty rascals."

"I would have thought of him as king of the dirty rascals," I said dryly.

"That sounds about right," Tully agreed. "But his family looked out for me when my family didn't. You might say I owe them. Sooner or later, Reuben is going to remember that and come calling for a favour."

"He hasn't already? He asked me to try to talk Zeke out of leaving the band. He didn't want you to do the same thing?" I swallowed the last gulp of wine and mopped up my sauce with a piece of garlic bread.

"Reuben is smart enough to know I wouldn't do that, and Zeke wouldn't listen to me if I did," Tully said. "It's not in my best interest to try to convince him to walk away. Whereas with you, you could make a future with Zeke away from the band. You might even have considered that once the tour is over."

"I hadn't. Not yet anyway," I said. That made a twisted kind of sense though. Reuben was trying to get to Zeke through me and vice versa. "At some point, we might have to think about life after music, but not for a while. Not while Wolf Venom is selling out stadiums all over the world. Why doesn't Reuben just wait until that happens?

"Firstly, it's not going to happen," Tully said with a confident smile. "We're going to be selling out everywhere until we're too old to stand. And even if we didn't, Zeke doesn't want anything to do with that lifestyle. None of us do." He paused for a moment then added, "There's something else. Something you should know. I…" He rubbed the back of his head. "I hope this doesn't scare you off."

"After everything that's happened already, I'm not sure what you could possibly say that *would* scare me off," I said.

It would have to be pretty fucking bad. I was almost certain he wasn't about to admit he was the one leaving all those heads lying around. What could be scarier than that?

"You haven't heard what I have to say yet," he pointed out.

He sat forward and rested his chin in his hands. "When my adopted family took me in, they started to train me in my mother's profession."

It took me a solid minute to even begin to process what he was trying to say.

"Whoa." I sat back in my chair but had the presence of mind to speak softly. "You trained as an assassin?"

He glanced down at the table, then back up again. "Yeah. It's not a craft I practice now, and it's not something I'm proud of, but yes. They trained me in... all aspects of the job."

I felt the blood drain out of my face. "Have you ever—" Fuck did I even want to know the answer to that?

He looked back down at the table and for the longest time I didn't think he was going to respond. When he looked back up, I saw the answer in his eyes.

"So, yes?" Holy shit.

"Once, and like I said, it's not something I'm proud of. The job made me enough money to buy the kind of guitar I needed to join Wolf Venom when they were starting out. I know that's no excuse for what I did, but that was why I did it. For what it's worth, the guy was a powerful man who was using his position to get away with raping women and young girls. If I hadn't done it, someone else would have. And if they hadn't, he would have kept doing what he was doing."

I felt like I should have been horrified, but for

some reason, I wasn't. Tully was a good guy, and I could see that killing, even someone evil, weighed heavily on his mind.

But I had to ask. "The heads?"

He shook his head. "Not me. From what I saw of Poppy and Calista, it's not someone trained to have any finesse. Those two, at least, weren't professional hits. I doubt the other ones were either."

I wasn't sure if I had enough wine for this conversation. I wasn't sure if enough wine existed.

"So you have no interest in going back to that life?" I asked tentatively, even though I was sure of the answer.

"None," he said firmly. "That's in the past, much to my parents' disappointment."

"Good, because I can't imagine you as a hitman," I said. "You make a much better guitarist." That would explain why Brantley senior placed Tully where he did. He must have had a plan for him.

There was something wrong with me, because I found him hotter than ever, knowing he was a trained assassin. I mean, you don't meet people like that every day, much less go on dates with them. Knowing he had skills made me feel safer than ever.

"Ain't that the truth," he said lightly. "I'm not bothered by death, but I don't want to kill people for a living. Or even by accident. The previous generation must be shaking their heads at us."

"Yes, it's disappointing that you don't want to follow in their criminal footsteps," I said ironically. "Young people these days."

He grinned. "Right? With such delinquents. Imagine raising rock stars instead of thugs."

"Maybe there's hope for the world yet," I said.

6

ABBIE

"Okay," I said slowly, "this wasn't what I was expecting."

"What were you expecting?" Tully pressed his hand lightly to the small of my back. "Whips and chains hanging from the walls? A line of St Andrews crosses? A few sex chairs and a swing?"

"Ummm… Yes?"

I'd been to places like this before so yeah, that was pretty much what I thought I'd see here.

In reality, the club—Desdemona's—was plush and high-end. I suspected they catered to whatever their clients wanted. Including discretion.

The floors were white marble, the walls a soft blue. Dark blue couches lined the walls, broken up by deep armchairs and mahogany tables.

If I didn't know better, I'd assume we were in an expensive lawyer's office. That was probably the idea. If anyone walked past, they'd assume nothing interesting went on here. Unless you're the kind of person who finds legal stuff fun.

I mean, whatever floats your boat.

Tully chuckled. "I know a few places like that too, but Desdemona likes to make things more personal. When I booked, I gave her a list of what and how I wanted things for tonight."

I glanced at him in surprise. "You had to book?"

"Hell yeah, weeks in advance," he said. "Some people wait *months* to get in here."

"It helps to be a rock god." My gaze skimmed over several tasteful paintings on the walls. They were all landscapes, but not of anywhere I knew.

"Sometimes," he said unapologetically. "I don't usually throw my name around but how else am I going to impress you?"

"By being you?" I suggested.

Don't get me wrong, I liked that he was willing to make the effort to introduce me to his world and do it in a way I'd feel comfortable. And okay, I kinda didn't mind him throwing a little bit of weight around. He wasn't the kind of guy who would do it often, and not without good cause. He was no Vance or even Penn.

"I'm awesome," he said with a grin, "but I'd like to be awesome on the next level tonight. Fuck knows how long it'll be until I have you to myself again. If I make this memorable enough, it might be sooner."

"You make it sound like you need to fight the other guys for a chance to be with me," I said. That wouldn't end well for anyone.

"Whatever I have to do," he said in a light, teasing tone. "Hey, Desdemona." He greeted the woman who appeared through a side door.

She was absolutely stunning. Tall, almost as tall as Tully, and more curvaceous than me. Her skin was the darkest brown I ever saw. She held herself like a woman who knew exactly how gorgeous she was. She owned every centimetre of it, from her long legs to the cleavage that pressed up from the front of her bright red dress.

"Mr Cole." She glided forward and kissed him on both cheeks before she did the same to me.

"Miss Hart. So wonderful to have you both here. I have everything arranged precisely as you asked." She gave me a look that suggested it absolutely mattered who I was. Not as Abbie Hart, the singer, but as a welcome, cherished guest.

No wonder people liked to come here. Pun intended.

"Thank you, Desdemona." Tully kissed her cheeks in return.

I hesitated before I did the same. Her skin was smooth and cool under my lips, soft compared to kissing any of the guys.

"Please, come through." She gestured toward the door she'd come out of with hands coated in gold rings and dripping with diamonds. There must be money to be made in owning a place like this.

What was I saying? If there was a golden rule in this life, it was that sex sells.

His hand still on the small of my back, Tully guided me through the doorway and into a small but opulent room with a view over the Swan River.

I was so busy gaping at the wide, four poster bed and silver covered tray that sat on the top of the table beside it, that I didn't notice Desdemona leave until the door closed behind us.

"This is next level all right," I said in awe.

The floor was a dark hardwood, no doubt easy to clean, but expensive. Even the curtains hanging on the windows looked like they cost more than a pretty penny.

"Is that wallpaper on the ceiling?" It looked like marble with gold veining running through it.

"Yes, and jets in the bath." Tully gestured.

My gaze followed where he pointed and I did a double take.

"I didn't even see that." Which was bizarre since it was the biggest, longest, widest clawfoot tub I ever saw. The sides were painted a glossy black while the tub itself was a glistening white. Steam rose off water inside the tub, which was decorated with a sprinkle of rose petals.

"This feels like the honeymoon I never had." I shook my head in amazement. "You asked for all of this?"

"Everything," he said. "She has a room which is completely black and no light can get inside. It heightens all the rest of your senses. It's incredible, but I thought maybe for your first time here, I'd ease you into it."

"I appreciate that," I said. Even trusting him the way I did, to be in complete darkness sounded freaky. That was definitely something I'd have to work up to.

"Now remember, you're in charge of this," he said. "I'm here to guide you and help you enjoy the experience, but you get to say when something is too much or too little. Okay?"

I nodded. "Okay. Where do we start?" I was hoping he had some ideas, because I could easily get overwhelmed right now. Just imagining what was on the tray, under the cover, made my mind race.

"Why don't we start by sitting down?" He waved toward the bed. "Let me try a few things and see what you like. And if you need to tap out, just say the word."

"Any word?" I asked. "Or, like, cucumber or something?"

He grinned. "Cucumber works. If you need or want me to stop, just say that, okay?"

"All right," I agreed. I sat down on the edge and watched as he picked up a red, silk blindfold off the table beside the tray.

"Can I put this on you?" he asked.

I hesitated for a short while.

Did I trust him enough to let him do things to me I couldn't see?

Yeah, yeah I did. More than that, the idea got my heart racing.

I sat around to face away from him and said, "Yes please."

He slipped the smooth fabric over my eyes and

fastened it in place. "Any time you want to take that off, go ahead. You're in control of that too."

I pulled out a section of hair where it was caught up in the fabric and nodded.

"Okay. I'm good for now." I couldn't see, but the fabric wasn't so thick that I was completely devoid of all light. "Thank you for being sweet."

"I was going to say the same to you," he said. "Now, I'm going to put something to your lips, but it won't be anything horrible. All right?"

"I trust you," I said.

"Good," he said. "Here's the first thing."

I heard the rattle of the cover lifting off the tray and he pressed something cool to my lips. I breathed in the delicious scent of strawberry. One of my favourite foods.

I slid my tongue against it, felt the rough skin of the fruit, tasted the flavour for a moment before I took a bite.

"Yum." I couldn't remember eating a tastier one. It could have just been picked, it was so fresh.

"Yes, you are," he agreed. He waited until I opened my mouth wider before popping the rest of the strawberry into my mouth.

I chewed and swallowed, then waited. "That was a good start. What else you got?"

He chuckled. "That's my girl. Let's try..." He rattled around before he lightly pressed something hard against my lips.

I breathed in the smell. It didn't take long to identify what it was.

"Mmmm, chocolate." I licked it eagerly. And kept licking and nibbling when it became evident he wasn't going to pop it into my mouth. I ate right down to the tips of his fingers and licked those as well. After a moment, he popped one into my mouth and let me suck.

"You're even tastier than strawberries and chocolate," I said.

"You too." The next thing he pressed against my mouth were his lips, but the kiss he gave was soft and brief. "Can I take off your dress?" he asked.

At this point, I was pretty sure there wasn't anything he could do to me I wouldn't like. What can I say, I'm easily won over by strawberries and chocolate.

Not to mention smoking hot rock gods like Tully.

"Please." I turned around again so he could work the zip down and tug the straps of my shoulders. The fabric slid against my skin down to my waist before he took my hand and encouraged me to stand. When my dress fell in a pool at my feet, I stepped out of it and shoved it aside with my toe.

"Black lace, my favourite," he remarked.

"Oh, it is?" I filed that in the back of my mind for future reference.

Asher and Zeke liked my white lace bras and panties, although I think they preferred me without any underwear. The feeling was mutual.

"Okay, let's try something different," he said.

I listened for the sound of him rattling around, but it didn't come. Nothing touched my lips. For a while, I started to think he wasn't doing anything.

"What—" Then I felt a light touch on my cheek, down my neck to my throat.

The edge of a feather.

I shivered slightly. "That tickles."

He paused the moment I spoke. "Do you want me to stop?"

"No," I said quickly. "It's not a bad tickle."

"Okay, great." He continued to run it lightly over my neck and down my chest.

For some reason, that slight touch was incredibly erotic. It was soft and gentle and made my skin tingle all over.

He slid the feather down between my breasts and over my stomach. He ran it back up and over one nipple, barely touching through the fabric of my bra.

I groaned softly. This might be the longest, slowest tease ever, and it was going to drive me completely wild. I loved every moment of it.

He passed the feather over the other nipple and back down across my stomach, over the side of my thigh and down one leg. He brought it up the inside of my thigh which I opened eagerly, my body already begging for more.

When I wanted him to touch my pussy, he moved in the opposite direction.

"Let's try something different," he mused. "Hmmm. Ahhh." He must have put the feather away, because the next time he touched my mouth, it was with something so cold it made me jump slightly.

"Is that okay?" he asked.

"Yeah," I said immediately. "I wasn't expecting ice." The sudden increase in sensation wasn't unpleasant, just different.

"Great." He pressed the cube to my lips and let me lick before he slid it down my cheek and across my throat. It left behind an ache that I wanted to feel all over.

He didn't disappoint. He let the cube slide down my chest and over my nipple.

If it wasn't hard before, it was after the shock of the cold over my sensitive nub. It left the fabric of my bra wet and freezing against my skin.

"I never knew ice could feel so good," I whispered.

"It's surprising what you can feel when you can't see and you don't make expectations," he said. "Everything is…"

"More?" I suggested.

"Yes, more," he agreed. The ice cube must have all but melted before he passed it over my opposite nipple, leaving that bra cup drenched as well.

I shivered, but it was with need, not with cold.

"I see why you like this," I said. "Pun not intended."

He laughed softly and said, "Stick out your tongue." When I did, he put the last small chip of ice on my tongue.

It melted away in a second or two, leaving a drop of cold water, which I swallowed.

"Let's try something else," he said. "Lie down on your stomach."

I did, with my hands out to either side of my face. I thought he was going to use the feather again, but when he touched me it felt more substantial.

"Is that—"

"It's a flogger," he said. "I'll start gently."

"I trust you," I said again.

I felt the brush of multiple strands of butter soft leather swipe over the back of my wrist. I turned my hand to let it run smoothly over the underside of my fingers and the pads of my fingertips.

He ran it slowly and gently up my arm, over my elbow to my shoulder. From there, he traced lines slowly up and down my back and over my ass.

I shivered as every touch increased my arousal. We'd barely done anything and I was as turned on as hell. And still mostly dressed. I was definitely a convert to Tully's sensation play. It was next level and then some.

"Can I unhook your bra?" he asked.

"Please." I wasn't sure if I was agreeing or begging for more. Maybe both. My whole body was on fire in the best possible way.

He released the hooks and the fabric sprang apart.

"Your skin is so beautiful." I felt the brush of his lips on my back before he worked his way up to my shoulders. The bed moved as he sat up and started to trace lines up and down from the back of my neck to the top of my panties with the flogger.

"Mmm, Tully. Can you do that a little harder?" I said breathlessly.

"Absolutely I can," he agreed. He brought the flogger down on the skin of my lower back hard enough to leave a slight sting.

The jolt of heat that went all the way through my body was insane.

Holy shit. Somehow he knew just the right amount of pressure to use.

"Is that all right?" he asked.

"Mmm, more than all right," I said. "Can you do that again? Please."

"Of course."

And he did, three or four more times, before I had to say, "Harder, please."

The stinging slap of the leather against my skin was absolute perfection. If foreplay was an art, then he was an artist.

"Oh God, yes, that." I moaned. "Again, please."

He brought it down several more times, before he stopped. "Your skin is the most beautiful shade of pink. Let's try something else, shall we?"

"Yes, yes, anything," I said. I didn't even care at that point, as long as he did *something* to me.

"Can I take off your panties?" he asked.

"Yes please," I said immediately. I lifted my hips to

let him hook his fingers into the waistband. He slid them down my legs and off my feet.

As much as anything else he was doing to me, I loved that he stopped to check back with me at every step. His middle name might be consent.

For a trained assassin, he was the master of respect. I adored him all the more for it.

I listened carefully, trying to figure out what he'd do next. I was tempted to peek, but the anticipation was half the excitement.

"I'm going to let you feel this first," he said. "Turn your hand over so your palm is upward. Please."

Because he asked so nicely, and because I wanted to, I turned my hand over.

He ran something firmer, but still smooth, over my skin. Something round, with a flat surface. Curious, I brought over my other hand and felt three flaps of leather which were attached to a handle.

"A paddle?" I guessed.

"Yes," he said. "And because you guessed right, I'm going to use it on you. If that's all right?"

"I'll be disappointed if you don't." Honestly, I couldn't fucking wait. My ass was singing out for his attention. The rest of me wasn't far behind.

"I don't want to disappoint you." Like he did with a feather and the flogger, he ran the paddle lightly over my skin first, touching me all over before he gave me a slight slap on the palm of my hand.

The sections of paddle cracked against each other. The sound and touch was like lightning shooting through me. I was so wet from it, I was drenched.

"I'm going to use this on your ass now," he said. "I'm going to make you nice and pink there too." The bed moved as he shuffled down.

"Come here." He put a hand in mine and guided me up onto all fours. He slipped my still damp bra off the rest of the way. "Hold on to the bedpost."

He pressed my palm against the cool timber until I curled the fingers of both hands around it.

I stuck out my ass and scrunched up my face in anticipation of the pain, but the sting was only slightly more intense than on my hand.

"Again, please." I didn't ask for him to do it harder, not yet. The slap of the paddle was so different to the flogger, it was a sensation in itself.

Two, three more times he slapped the paddle down on my bare skin. Never in exactly the same place. Each time sent a spectacular burst of pain and desire through me. I was so hot I was about ready to hump the bed post.

"Tully," I said with what little voice I could muster. "I want you. Please."

"Loveliness, I want you too." He must have tossed the paddle onto the tray because it landed with a clatter.

He knelt beside me and cupped my ass with his hands. Slowly and deliberately, he slid his calloused fingers around my cheeks and up my back. When he reached my sides, he slipped his hands underneath me, over my stomach and up under my breasts.

I wanted to see him, but at the same time I only wanted to feel him touch me. For now, I left the blindfold in place.

He slid his hands up between my breasts and up to my face. He traced circles around the still fading bruises on my cheek before he kissed my mouth.

He tasted lightly of beer and garlic from the dinner we shared. His upper lip and chin were rough with a few days' worth of growth of stubble. His mouth, so wide and generous, felt like he might devour me.

I'd let him.

He drew me away from the bedpost and onto my back beside him.

My hands free of the bedpost, I let my hands wander over him. At some point during all of this, he'd shed his clothes. It almost didn't seem fair that I couldn't see him naked, but what I felt was pretty fucking impressive.

His body was firm and hard, ripples of muscle, slanted here and there with scars and dips where his skin moulded over his bones.

"You feel amazing," I said between luscious, deep kisses.

"No, you," he said. He broke off from my mouth and kissed down the side of my jaw to my throat. From there, he slowly worked his way down to my breasts.

Both of them were aching to be touched. By the time he slid his tongue over my nipple, my whole body was ready to scream.

Instead, I huffed a breath out through my nose and ran my fingernails over his back.

"You can do that harder if you like," he said between licks. "Leave some scratch marks."

While he mercilessly licked and sucked my nipples, I did just that, digging my nails into his skin until he groaned with pleasure.

Eventually, and I sensed with reluctance, he kissed and licked his way further down my body. He teased my belly button with the tip of his tongue and made me giggle.

"That tickles," I protested, but not too hard.

He chuckled and moved down until his stubble grazed the inside of my thighs.

I shivered with delicious anticipation.

Anticipation he drew out as long as he could, by kissing his way down to my knees and back up the other thigh.

"You are such a tease," I complained.

"I like to take my time," he said unapologetically. Still, he gently bent my knee and, lighter than a feather, lapped the tip of his tongue over the hood of my clit.

I didn't hesitate to say, "Harder, please."

"Yes ma'am." He lapped firmer now, his tongue deliberate and skilled. He played me as well as he played any of his guitars, with care and attention, obviously watching for my reactions so he knew what I liked.

I liked it all, especially when he slipped a couple of firm, rough fingers inside me.

"You're wetter than the bath," he said.

"I bet I am," I said. I was so fucking aroused I could barely think straight. "I'm going to come."

"Please do." He went on working me until a peak of pleasure rushed over me.

I curled my fingers into the bedcovers and

bucked against his mouth. The orgasm was hard and fast, with the promise of only being the first of many.

He waited until I came down before he slid his fingers out of me. The bed moved and I found something else pressed against my lips. His fingers, slick with my juices.

"How does this taste?" When I opened my mouth, he slipped them inside and let me suck. The taste of his skin and my arousal was delicious.

"If I could bottle it, I would make a fortune," I said around his fingertips. When he slipped them back out, I added, "I want you inside me. Please"

"Gladly," he said. His voice was rough with desire. He rolled me over on my side so I was facing him, and drew one of my legs over his hip.

I felt his erection against my thigh before he pressed the tip into the entrance of my pussy. He stayed like that for at least a minute or two.

"I want to enjoy every second of this," he whispered. "You're so fucking worth the wait."

"So are you," I said.

Just as I started to think he was going to stay like that forever, he slid in deeper and let out a soft groan.

Again he went still for a minute or two before he

started to move with slow, intense strokes. There was nothing frantic or hurried about his movements. He slid all the way to his balls, then all the way back to his tip, drawing out each thrust.

"You feel incredible." He filled me to the brim with his cock. He must have had a piercing, I felt something smooth nudge my g-spot with each thrust.

"You don't feel so bad yourself." I couldn't take it anymore. "Can you take this off, please?" I needed to see him, to watch his hard body move as he fucked me.

"Of course."

The blindfold slipped off my eyes and I blinked at the sudden light and his soft smile.

Just as I suspected, his body was all muscles, tattoos and scars.

Holy shit, he was hot.

"You're beautiful," I told him.

"No, you." He grunted and his breath quivered. "I'm going to come. Can I come inside your gorgeous body?"

"Oh, fuck, yes please." I was on the edge again myself before he asked. Afterward, I was absolutely out-of-my-mind aroused.

He thrust a little faster now and slipped his hand

down between us to rub my clit. A few strokes was all it took to have me quivering and shattered on the end of his fingers and cock.

As if me coming drew his orgasm out of him, Tully came too, grunting and bucking against me, balls grinding, prolonging the pleasure for us both.

Finally we fell in a tangle of arms, legs and sweat. I lay there panting until my head cleared and I caught my breath.

"That was... Wow." I exhaled long and low.

"Just the beginning," he said. "The bath should still be warm enough. Let me clean you up."

ABBIE

WHAT THE FUCK?" I stared at the photo on the screen.

I was a little sore and tired from the night before, so I'd left Tully to sleep and had a quick shower before getting dressed in a tee and track pants. A lazy start to the day called for casual clothes.

While the kettle heated up for a much needed coffee, I picked up my phone to scroll through social media.

The first thing I saw after a picture of someone's cat, was a photo of the guys in the restaurant last night. They looked like they had a good time. They were smiling and laughing with a group of other people. No one I recognised.

I smiled in response to their infectious smiles.

Even in candid photos, they were hot and charismatic. And mine.

I scrolled on down the feed and froze.

"What the—"

In the next photo, Penn was sitting with a woman on his lap.

Okay, that was cool. We weren't together like I was with Zeke, Asher and Tully. He could do what he wanted, with whomever he wanted, whenever he wanted.

Then why the fuck did it bother me so much?

All right, I admit it, I enlarged the photo for a better look at her. Who was she?

Probably a random fan of the band. From the look on her face, she was having the time of her life. Penn looked indifferent, but he wasn't pushing her off.

Whatever, come on, Abbie. Let it go. He's made it clear he's not interested in you. Why shouldn't he hook up with her?

I knew the answer to that. Right or wrong, I was drawn to the guy. I wanted him, even now. Fuck, I was jealous.

I needed to get a grip.

I pinched the screen back to the normal size and went on scrolling.

I froze again.

What the absolute mother-loving fuck?

The next photo on my feed was one of all of the guys. They sat at a table in the restaurant, empty plates in front of them. Landon and Channing had their arms looped around each other. Penn had the same woman on his lap.

Asher and Zeke each had a woman on their laps.

My heart stopped.

Like the woman on Penn's lap, these two looked like they were having a shit ton of fun. Each had an arm around the guys' shoulders, their cheeks pressed to theirs, and were smiling at the camera.

The guys were grinning like they were out on a date with their girlfriends.

"What the fuck?" I said under my breath.

"What is it?" Tully was standing near the hotel phone, looking at the room service menu. I hadn't even noticed him get out of bed.

If I wasn't so floored, I would have taken the time to appreciate how beautifully naked he was.

Instead, I rose from the chair I was perched on and walked over to show him my phone.

His eyebrows rose. "Oh." For a while that seemed to be all he could say. Then finally, "I'm sure there's a perfectly good explanation."

"I'm sure there is," I said wryly. "Like when I'm not around, they do shit like this?" They hadn't even tried to hide it. They knew the camera was on them.

"Abbie—" Tully put a hand on my arm. "Do me a favour and don't jump to conclusions until we've spoken to them. If this shit is how it looks, then we'll deal with it."

"Are you going to kill them for me?" I was joking.

Mostly.

Ish.

"Maybe after the tour." Evidently, he wasn't ruling it out either.

Okay, I didn't want them dead and he was right, there might be a perfectly reasonable explanation for it, but the photos still made me incredibly uncomfortable. How would they feel if I was sitting in a strange guy's lap, smiling at the camera? As jealous as I felt right now, wouldn't they?

"I was going to order us breakfast, but would you prefer to go down and eat in the restaurant with them?" he asked gently.

It was completely unfair that I was standing in a hotel room in Perth with a gloriously gorgeous, naked rock god who paddled my ass last night, and all I could think of was a bunch of stupid photos. I should be enjoying my time here with him.

"We'll get lots of other chances," he said as though he read my mind. He drew me into his arms and slowly kissed my mouth.

"When you put it that way," I slipped my arms around his neck, "maybe we could go back to bed instead? We don't have to be at the soundcheck for a while. There's plenty of time to fit in breakfast somewhere in there."

My irritation didn't completely melt away, but I wasn't going to ruin this time between us with what might be jealousy over nothing. If there was something to it, I'd fucking deal with it later.

"I know better than to argue with a beautiful woman." Tully pushed my track pants down until they dropped to the floor. My panties went next, while I pulled off my shirt and bra that I'd only worn for about five minutes.

Oh well, it was good while it lasted.

"When did you get so enlightened?" I asked.

He cupped my ass, then slid his hands down lower to hoist me up until my legs wrapped around his waist. He carried me over to the bed and lowered me down. He lay down beside me before grabbing me and rolling me so I was full length on top of him.

He grinned up at me. "When I realised not

arguing was more likely to lead to you lying on top of me just like this."

"Oh." I kissed his wide mouth. "You have it all figured out." I kissed him again.

"You better believe I do," he said. "It was all part of my nefarious plan."

"Nefarious?" I echoed. "I don't know, but I think it might be too early in the day, and we haven't had enough caffeine, for a word like that. What does that even mean?"

He chuckled. "I'm not exactly sure, but it probably applies to me. It sounded like a good fit."

"Speaking of a good fit…" I reached between us and curled my hand around his already erect cock.

My fingers found the warm metal of what I now knew was a reverse Prince Albert piercing, and slotted in under the barbell.

He explained he got it to make himself suffer for killing a man for money, but it felt so good inside me. That might be wrong on some level, but I couldn't bring myself to care right now.

Just the thought of it was enough to make me fucking wet.

As soon as he was fully hard, I placed my hands on his chest and lowered my pussy down onto his cock. With a little manoeuvring, his piercing massaged by g-spot. My clit slapped against the base of his stomach.

"Why did you get the reverse Prince Albert not the Prince Albert?" I asked, my eyes half closed.

He smiled at me and reached up to run his hands lightly over my breasts.

"Because this works better for face-to-face. I like to look at you. To know you feel good. And I get to see your gorgeous breasts. It seemed like all the winning to me."

"Me too." I rode him slowly. How funny that something he did as punishment to himself brought a ton of pleasure to me. I tried not to think about that in a way, a man died for this. If Tully said he deserved it, I believed him.

And the sex was really, really good.

I closed my eyes fully, and like I did the night before, surrendered to sensation and stopped thinking too much about things that didn't matter right now. The only thing that mattered was here and now, this moment, our two bodies sliding together, the delicious friction created between us.

"You are the most incredible woman," he said so softly I almost missed hearing him say it.

"You're incredible yourself," I whispered back. I thought I was satisfied last night, enough to keep me for a while, but I was quickly hurtling towards a beautiful abyss where I would happily stay forever if I could.

My hands curled and I raked my nails lightly over his chest. The marks I left there now would match the ones on his back.

I wanted to cling to him forever, to make this moment last, but I couldn't hold back the orgasm that rushed over me. It made my blood thunder through my body like a tsunami of pleasure with a few bolts of lightning and some fireworks thrown in for good measure.

I threw back my head and cried towards the ceiling.

As if the sound pushed him over the edge, Tully came, thrusting harder and harder into me, his breath a series of ragged grunts. His hands gripped my breasts to the point of exquisite pain. It drew my orgasm out longer, until I felt like my body might be completely sucked dry of every drop of pleasure.

Only when it was done was I able to start to catch my breath, a little bit of reality came crashing back in.

I was going to have to deal with the other guys and those photos.

8

ABBIE

I DIDN'T NEED a mirror to know my expression was grim when I stepped into the hotel room the other guys were sharing.

Tully followed me in, a hand on my shoulder for reassurance.

"I was wondering when you two would appear," Asher said lightly. "Did you have a nice time?" He didn't even look slightly guilty.

Should I be more worried than I was, or less?

"Yes, it was lovely," I said vaguely. "How about you guys?" If they did something to piss me off, I hoped they'd admit to it now.

This was their chance, before I asked about the photos.

"It was about the usual," Zeke said. "Dinner and a

few drinks. Nothing exciting." He also didn't look guilty. He got up from the chair he was sitting in and pushed his phone into his pocket.

Considering their *usual* seemed to involve a different groupie every night, his words weren't encouraging. Maybe they were so desensitised to it that they didn't see anything wrong with it.

"Nothing exciting, huh?" Tully stepped out from behind me and crossed his arms over his chest.

"No new heads," Landon said.

"Thank fuck," Penn muttered.

That was something, I suppose. We had all survived the night.

"Are you okay, love?" Asher asked. "You look a little pale. Did Tully go too hard?" He looked worried, but at the same time, like he was trying not to smile.

"No, Tully was fine," I said absently. "More than fine," I added when I realised I might have made him sound inadequate. "Like I said, it was lovely."

Zeke frowned and looked from Tully to me and back again. "Okay, what's going on? Did you two get married or something?"

"Oh, hell no," I said immediately. I was never going to do that again with anyone.

At least, I couldn't *imagine* doing it again. Not

even with any of these guys. Relationships were so much more than a piece of paper. I didn't need that to know I was loved.

But—was I loved?

"We saw some photos of you guys online," Tully said.

Every single face stared at us with a blank, confused look.

It was Asher who broke the silence with, "Penn, have you been posting dick pics online again?"

Penn snorted. "If I posted pics of my cock online, they would break the internet with my awesome-ness." After a moment he added, "That would be a no."

"We figured," Asher said.

"What photos are you talking about, sweetheart?" Zeke asked me.

I cocked my head at him, but he seemed genuinely confused. That or he was a good actor. What line had he spun for the woman on his lap?

I pulled out my phone and switched on the screen. I found the last photo and turned my phone around to show him.

He leaned forward and peered at it. His eyebrows twitched, but that was the only sign of any kind of emotion.

"Oh, that." He was still completely unworried.

"Yes, that." I tilted the screen so all the guys could take a look.

Penn seemed the most interested. "See, I don't even need to share photos of my cock. I look pretty fucking good right there." He gestured towards my phone, palm upward.

"That's a good angle for you," Asher agreed.

I lowered my hand. "Really? That's all you have to say about it? What about the fact there are women sitting on your laps, their hands all over you?"

They all frowned at me. Did they really not understand why I might be pissed off? Apparently they didn't. Was I not being clear or did they not give a shit?

"Right," I said finally. I tucked my phone into my pocket. "Of course. It's no big deal. You met some women and hooked up like you've done, what? A thousand times before? No big deal."

Only, it *was* a big deal. I felt like they'd stabbed me through the heart and twisted the knife. It wasn't even a nice, quiet assassination while I slept. It was yet another, very public act, and it was humiliating. It dredged up a bunch of old—okay not that old —heartbreak.

Those feelings were more raw than I expected.

Now confronted by them, I realised I hadn't put them behind me as well as I thought. I felt like I was starting to unravel, just when I thought my life was back on track.

I should have known I couldn't put all the shit of my past behind me. Whatever happened and wherever I went, I kept making stupid fucking decisions. Was trusting these guys yet another one?

Right now my brain was topsy-turvy and I wanted to throw up.

Asher laughed.

Laughed.

I swung my face around and glared at him.

None of this was okay. I was angry and he thought it was funny. What the fuck? Maybe I didn't know him at all.

"What's so funny?" I demanded. "I thought you cared about me." Fuck, now I was going to cry in front of them. I blinked back tears that threatened to slide down my face.

Fucking hell.

"We didn't hook up with any of them." It was Zeke who responded. "You have no idea who they are?"

"Should I?" I asked. Demanded.

"I don't have a clue," Tully said.

"Ohhh, I get it," Asher drawled. "No, it's definitely *not* what you think. Those women, they're Cameo Orchid. They just signed with White Wolf Records. They're doing a small tour and happened to be in town the same time as us. Jackson introduced us and suggested we take some photos as publicity for them."

He made it all sound perfectly reasonable.

"Jackson suggested they sit on your laps?" My voice sounded colder than I intended, but his words barely made a dent in my emotions..

"No. That was their idea," Asher said lightly. "We…" He exchanged glances with Zeke. "We didn't think there was any harm in it."

"We would have told you, but you were busy with Tully," Zeke said, as if that magically made everything all right. As if it was okay to make this Tully's and my fault.

Zeke looked at me intently. "Like Asher said, it wasn't a big deal. It was just a couple of photos for publicity. Jackson took the photos. I'm sure he'd show you the rest if you want to have a look. They'll show you nothing went on."

"Did they know it was just for publicity?" I asked. "This… Cameo Orchid? Because they seemed awfully comfortable."

I sounded like a jealous bitch, but it went deeper than that. I believed them when they said nothing happened, but there was more to it. Something apparently none of them considered.

"Jazz tried to touch my cock," Penn said. He shrugged like it was an everyday occurrence. Maybe it was.

Zeke and Asher exchanged confused glances again.

"Like we said, it was their idea," Zeke said. "The whole thing was over faster than Penn getting himself off."

Penn flipped him the bird. "I'm not that quick, asshole."

"But the photos were," Asher said. "I promise you, that was all there was. Just a couple of publicity photos."

"Photos designed to make the public think you guys are with these women," I said. "Photos designed to generate gossip. Photos designed to boost their popularity because people think they each managed to snag a member of Wolf Venom, even if it's just for a night."

I watched their faces as the penny started to drop. They should all know by now how I felt about using fake relationships to make and sell a person's image.

"I can see how it might be construed that way," Zeke said carefully. "That wasn't my intention."

"No, but it was probably theirs," I agreed. "But you guys went along with it. And so did Jackson. He of all people should know better."

They all fucking should. Hot tears prickled the corners of my eyes.

"To be fair to Jackson, his job is to sell all of us," Zeke said reasonably. "Sometimes that means doing shit like this."

"Are you okay with that?" I asked. "Would you be okay with it if Jackson told you to marry one of them, just for publicity?"

Zeke looked at me in shock. "Fuck no. There's a big difference between that and having someone sit on your lap."

"Is there?" The expression on his face made me wonder if I was overreacting, but after the way I was used, I didn't want it to happen to anyone else, the guys, or another band.

"You're still presenting a fake relationship to the public," I said. "Those photos are very... I don't know. It looks like you're dating them." I twisted the knife into my own heart by saying that out loud.

Zeke stepped towards me and put out his hand,

but I moved away. I was too pissed to let him touch me.

"Abbie—" He lowered his hand and sighed in frustration. "Sweetheart, you know what this business is like. Most of what the public sees is fake."

I knew that, I really did, but I didn't have to like it.

"Is it any different when you take a selfie with someone?" Zeke reasoned. "Don't you make it look like you're friends?"

"No, I don't," I said. "I certainly don't sit on anyone's laps. Not if it's someone I'm not in a relationship with."

"So you're jealous they were sitting on our laps and you weren't?" Penn asked. He shook his head and sneered.

"That's beside the point," I said.

"Is it?" He crossed his arms over his chest. "I think that's the whole point. You thought you had those two pussy whipped," he waved his fingers towards Asher and Zeke, "and you can't handle one little publicity shot with another woman. How are you going to handle it when they have photos taken with backing singers? You know they have photos taken with fans, don't you?"

"Of course I do," I spluttered. "That's beside the point—"

"It's exactly the point," he said evenly. "Our lives don't revolve around you twenty-four hours a day, seven days a week. And you *hate* that." He took a step towards me. "And you know what else you hate? You hate the fact you didn't realise what Vance did to you was a publicity stunt. You automatically want to assume every woman is as clueless as you. But they weren't. They knew exactly what was going on. And you know what? They enjoyed it, and so did we. *All of us.*"

I gaped. This was nasty, even for him.

I looked him right in the eyes and said, "Fuck you."

Through a haze of tears I turned and yanked open the hotel room door.

"Abbie—" One of the guys called out after me. I didn't know who and I didn't care right now.

I let the door bang shut behind me and headed down the stairs and away from the hotel.

9

TULLY

"Fucking hell, Penn," Zeke growled at the keyboardist.

I glared daggers at the man. Did he really need to be such an asshole?

Penn shrugged. "What about that wasn't true?"

"The part where you made it sound like we were fucking them," Asher growled.

"We were innocent bystanders," Landon pointed out.

Channing nodded his agreement.

"It was fucking innocent," Zeke said. He ran a hand over his hair. "But I'm starting to wish we'd said no to doing it."

"Why?" Penn scoffed. "Because you're as pussy

whipped as I said you were? Come off it, dude. It was no big deal until she made it a big deal. It's still not a big deal. It was one little fucking photo. We weren't rolling around naked in mud. If we were, it still wouldn't be a big deal. Not everything is Abbie's business."

"When are you going to admit you've fallen as hard for her as the rest of us?" I asked softly. "We all know it but you have to keep being a motherfucker and pretending you hate her guts."

He glared at me. "Has it ever crossed your mind that I *do* hate her guts, Tull?"

"No," I replied. "But it's crossed my mind she might hate yours if you keep behaving like a shit-head. I'm going after her."

Without waiting for a response from him, I grabbed the door handle and jerked it open.

"I'm going with you," Asher said.

"Me too." Zeke was right behind us. "You three stay here in case she comes back. If she does, let us know."

Penn grunted something.

I suspected he had no intention of coming with us anyway. That was fine by me. He'd done enough damage.

"Will do," Landon said. "Keep in touch with us.

I'm scared for her with a killer out there. What if they get to her next?"

"They won't," Channing said firmly. "She'll be fine. They'll find her." He gave Landon a hug and a quick kiss on the mouth.

I let the door swing shut behind us and hurried towards the elevator. Of course, it was on the ground floor so we had to press the button and wait for it to come back up to us.

"It might be quicker to take the stairs," Asher pointed out when the elevator was on the floor below ours.

"Too late now." Zeke shrugged. A couple of seconds later, a ping echoed through the corridor and the doors slid open.

We stepped inside and Asher turned to face me as the doors slid shut.

"Are you pissed off at us too, Tull?" he asked. "It seemed like a good idea at the time."

I shrugged. "It is what it is. If I was there, I would have posed with the rest of you. When Abbie calms down, she'll realise she would have done the same thing."

"Maybe." Asher looked uncertain. "But it wouldn't have happened at all if Abbie was there. We would have stood, a group of musos, hanging out together."

"Abbie was right," Zeke said slowly. "People will assume shit. That includes Reuben, and the killer."

"Unless they're the same person," Asher pointed out.

"Yes, unless Reuben hired the killer," Zeke agreed. "Either way, they could go after Cameo Orchid to get at the label or at us, or think they're getting rid of another of Abbie's enemies. Now was a stupid fucking time to get chummy with anyone." He looked furious with himself.

"Anyone could go to the White Wolf Records website to see who else they've signed," I pointed out. "If they wanted to go after the label, they don't need a photo."

If the killer wasn't after the label then yeah, the guys potentially made the other band a target.

"Can we blame Jackson?" Asher asked lightly.

"Only partially," Zeke said. "Mostly it was us not thinking, and getting caught up in the moment. We've done shit like that a thousand times before, but never when so much was at stake."

"Is this where you suggest leaving the band to keep us all safe?" Asher asked. "Because you know we're not letting you leave, right Tully?"

"Right," I agreed. "We're all in this together. And

fuck knows we can look after ourselves." We all had the skills to kill if we had to.

"Yeah, we can," Asher agreed. "But I've never been more tempted to hire you to take out Penn."

"I've never been so tempted to let you hire me," I said, only half joking.

"No one is taking a hit out on Penn," Zeke said. After a moment of expectant silence, he added, "If anyone is going to organise it, it will be me."

We all gave brief laughs. None of us would ever act on that, we just shared a dark, sometimes macabre sense of humour.

The elevator pinged and the doors opened on the ground floor.

I looked around the lobby, but saw no sign of Abbie.

The people behind the front desk had their eyes down on the computers. Those sitting in the café to the side of the lobby sipped their breakfast coffee without giving us more than a passing glance. A couple looked slightly disapproving at our torn jeans and faded T-shirts, not to mention the abundant tattoos we all had on display.

Evidently they thought the hotel was too fancy for scruffy rock stars.

Penn probably would have flipped them off and

told them he had more money than they did, but I just walked past like I belonged there.

Fuck them, I was as entitled to be there as they were.

Asher muttered something about entitled assholes, as we stepped out the front doors when they slid open for us.

It was another beautiful day in Perth. The sky was a striking blue and the air was warm. Summer was only a handful of weeks away. Tonight's concert was in an open roofed arena, and this was the perfect weather for it.

If we found Abbie in time to get there. A public whipping would be the least of our trouble if we missed it.

"I can't see her anywhere." Zeke stopped and turned a slow circle. "She couldn't have gotten too far."

I scanned the street around us, but saw no sign of the beautiful blond.

"She had her phone with her, let's try her on that," I said.

"Yes. Good idea." Zeke pulled out his phone and tapped at the screen. He put it to his ear and waited.

And waited.

"It's gone to voicemail. I guess she doesn't want to

talk to us yet." He ended the call and tapped at the screen again. "I'll send her a text. She'll know we're out here looking for her."

"If she looks at it," Asher said.

"She'll look at it when she's ready," I said.

"Maybe you should send her one," Asher said. "She's not pissed off at you."

"Or try calling," Zeke suggested.

I pulled out my phone and tried her number. It rang a few times but then went to voicemail.

"We're worried about you. Call me back." I ended the call and sent the same message via text. I watched until my phone said it was sent, then tucked it away in my pocket.

"Should we split up and look?" Asher asked.

Zeke shook his head. "I'm starting to get a bad feeling about this and I don't want anyone off by themselves."

"Same here." My spine tingled uncomfortably. All my senses were on high alert. I was trained to be observant, to take in every potential threat or observer that might cause me trouble. I leaned on that now.

"No one in the lobby seemed concerned," I said slowly. "There's no other way out without going via the front desk or the garage. The elevator came from the ground floor, so she didn't go through the garage."

Zeke nodded as he followed my reasoning. "When she came out of the elevator, she must have been walking, so no one paid attention to her."

"If she was running, the people in the lobby would still be reacting," Asher said.

"Exactly," I said. "So she got out here slowly, but then quickly disappeared out of sight. How does that happen?"

"A number of ways," Zeke said. "None of them good." He pulled out his phone. "Luckily I put a tracker on her phone, in case shit like this happened."

"Babe, you could have said that when we first got out here," Asher said.

"I just remembered," Zeke admitted. He squinted at his screen, then pointed down the street. "She's this way."

We followed him and his phone, but I kept all of my senses open. Would there come a day when I could completely relax and forget about my training? We were on tour, we should be enjoying ourselves, not worrying about threats and heads in boxes.

I wanted to agree with Channing's assumption

the killer wouldn't get to Abbie, but I wasn't so sure. They seemed to be getting more and more brazen. Taking Abbie right off the street might be their next step.

If that was the case, I would hunt them down and make them pay, and I wouldn't regret a second of it. I would make the motherfucker scream, not in a good way.

"Are you sure this is the right direction?" Asher asked. "Also, when did you get a chance to put a tracker on her phone?"

Zeke glanced up and grinned. "Back when she was staying in my place. After what happened with Jonah, I wanted to keep an eye on her. I would have put a tracker on her, but it's difficult to do without the person knowing about it."

Asher blinked at him a couple of times. "Where is it?"

"Where is what?" Zeke cocked his head and frowned.

"The tracker," Asher insisted. "Did you put one on me?" His hands hovered by his sides like he was ready to pat himself down to find it.

Zeke grinned. "Maybe I did, maybe I didn't."

While Asher stared at Zeke with wide eyes, I shook my head.

"You'd set off airport security if you had a tracker inside you," I said. "If he has a tracker on the rest of us, it's in our phones."

"Zeke?" Asher asked.

"I neither confirm nor deny," Zeke said. "This way. She's not far." He nodded in the direction of a small park maybe a hundred metres away.

It made sense for her to be there, clearing her thoughts. It was the kind of place I'd go too.

I squinted and scanned the area, but couldn't see any sign of her.

"She might be sitting under a tree," Asher suggested.

But she wasn't. We checked around every tree and even behind some bushes as we got closer to the tracker signal.

"It's just ahead," Zeke gestured. "Right… there."

A park bench sat under the shade of a tall gumtree. In the centre of the seat lay a phone.

In case there was any doubt, I pulled out my phone and pressed Abbie's number.

On the bench, the phone started to vibrate and play the start of one of our songs. Abbie's ringtone.

"That's hers all right," Asher said softly. He crept forward and picked up the phone as though he expected it to explode.

Honestly, I wouldn't have been surprised if it had. But it didn't.

Asher tapped the screen. "Missed messages and calls from us, but that's it. No numbers I don't recognise. Her phone doesn't seem to be damaged. It's like she put it down and walked off without it."

Zeke shook his head. "She wouldn't do that. She wouldn't risk anyone finding it and her personal photos."

I turned around and scanned the area. "Then where the fuck is she?"

10

ABBIE

I WOKE SLOWLY, with a pounding headache and crusty, dry eyes.

My mind was groggy and slow, but I acknowledged two things.

First, there was something over my eyes, like a blindfold or a scarf. Secondly, my wrists and ankles were bound.

It didn't feel like the fun Tully and I did—was it still just last night? I had no idea how much time had passed. It didn't feel like long, but it could have been days. Or longer. Had I missed any concerts?

Hell, why was that the first thing that popped into my head? What about the fact I was tied up by fuck knows who, who might not let me live for much longer?

That should worry me a shitload more than work.

"She's awake," a male voice said.

That gave me two more pieces of information. A man was involved and he wasn't alone. Unless he was talking to himself. That was confirmed a moment later when another voice spoke.

"So she is. I told you I didn't give her too much."

Too much what?

Memories came crawling back to me slowly, unpleasantly.

I walked out of the hotel like nothing was wrong. I didn't want to draw attention to myself. At the same time, I was trying not to cry.

Maybe I was overreacting about the photos, but Penn didn't need to be a prick about it. He certainly didn't need to imply I was a complete idiot because I didn't know what Vance planned.

I was naïve and in love, yeah, but not stupid. I saw the red flags, but I ignored every one of them. I wanted to believe he loved me too. There was nothing wrong with having faith in people.

Was there?

If Penn thought there was, then he could fuck off.

Once out on the street, I turned and walked in no particular direction. I found a small park and sat down on the bench. A guy came and sat beside me.

Memories came crashing back in, faster and more vivid now.

Hunter Brantley smiled at me. "Hey. Parker and I missed you."

I blinked at him in surprise. "What the fuck are you doing here?" The last time I saw Zeke's youngest, twin brothers, they dropped me off outside his house after they took me to speak to Reuben. At gunpoint. They were the last people I expected to see today. The last I wanted to see, except Penn.

"Shouldn't you be in school?" I asked.

"We're on holidays," Hunter said. "We thought we'd pop over to WA and say hi."

I didn't believe a single word of that. Still I gave him a fake smile and said, "Hi. I should be going."

The flicker of his eyes was the only warning I had that anyone was behind me. Before I could move, something clamped over my mouth. Cold, rough fabric, saturated with something that smelled medicinal and made my head spin.

"Not too much, Parker," Hunter said. "We don't want her asleep for too long."

Asleep? What the fuck?

In a matter of seconds, my eyes got heavy. I didn't know anything else until I woke up here.

"What do you want?" My voice was groggy but at least I wasn't gagged. Yet.

"Maybe we just want your company," Parker suggested. His voice was slightly deeper than Hunter's. That was the only way I could tell them apart.

"You could have asked." I struggled to sit up, but my head spun.

"Where's the fun in that?" Hunter asked cheerfully. He slid his hand up the inside of my thigh.

I shuddered and tried to pull away. Even if I wasn't half drugged, I wasn't strong enough to fight off both of them if they decided to rape me.

"Are you the ones killing people?" I asked. "Jonah. Vance." Those were the ones I knew the evil twins would know about. If they didn't know about the others, I wasn't going to tell them.

"I don't know, did we kill anyone Parker?" Hunter asked

"Recently?" Parker asked. "It's possible, but not Jonah."

"I don't think we killed Vance either, did we?" Hunter asked.

"No, I don't think so," Parker agreed. "Should we have?"

"It doesn't sound like it matters," Hunter said. "I mean, if he's dead already, then we don't need to do it."

"Good point," Parker said. "Plus Reuben doesn't like it if we kill people he doesn't tell us to kill."

"Did he tell you to kill me?" I asked. If they raped and killed me, they would have Zeke to answer to. And Asher and Tully at least. Maybe Landon and Channing too. Penn would probably find it funny. Asshole.

"Not yet," Parker said. "He sent us with a warning. He doesn't think Zeke or you took him seriously."

Hunter's fingers ghosted across the gusset of my panties. "He also wants to remind Zeke that he can reach him wherever he goes."

"We totally took him seriously." I was trying hard not to freak out. It wasn't the first time I'd been touched without my consent, but it was the most intimate. It was one thing to have my ass grabbed, but another to only have a thin sliver of fabric between Hunter's fingers and my pussy.

"I told him what Reuben said. You know what Zeke is like. He's not going to let me or anyone else dictate what he does."

"How hard did you try?" Hunter slid his fingers back the other way.

I swallowed and tried not to cry or give in to fear. "I don't know what you want me to say. I passed on the message. I can't make him leave Wolf Venom. The band is his life."

"Is that right?" A hand, I assumed it was Parker's, stroked over the side of my breast. "You must not be as close as we thought you were. What lengths would he go to, to keep you safe?"

I blinked away tears, glad now for the blindfold that stopped them from seeing them.

"Would he give up the band to save your life?" Hunter asked. His fingers stroked back the other way again.

"I don't know," I admitted. "He cares about me." I didn't mention that the last time I spoke to Zeke, I was angry at all of the guys except Tully. If the twins suspected we had any kind of fight, then my life might not be worth anything. I suspected they wouldn't kill me until they'd followed through with their implied threat of forcing themselves on me.

This day kept on getting better and fucking better, didn't it?

"You might need to impress upon him that he needs to make that choice," Hunter said. "You see how easy it was to get to you. How helpless you are right now. How vulnerable. Right now, Parker and I could do whatever we wanted to you and you would be powerless to stop us. You know that, right?"

"Yes." My voice came out in a squeak. I sounded like a terrified mouse.

Honestly, that was more or less accurate.

"I know that." Did I beg them not to, or did I remind them what their big brother would do to them if they harmed me? I didn't know if Zeke would give up the band, even for me, but I knew he would kick their asses into next year. He might even be tempted to let Tully use his skills on them. Or better yet, lock them in a room with Penn and his bullshit attitude.

Fingers lifted up the corner of the blindfold, before it was peeled off my face.

I blinked against the sudden glare. I lay in what looked like a hotel room, on a narrow bed. Judging by the way the sun was slanted in through the window, it was late afternoon. If it was still the same day, then I hadn't missed the concert yet.

I would like nothing more than to get there on time, alive and unraped.

Hunter smiled at me then took his hand out from under my skirt. "As much as we would like to have more fun with you, we don't have time. Besides, that will give you something to look forward to when we meet again. If Zeke hasn't listened by then."

"That's something to look forward to," I said sarcastically. My mind was a little clearer now, and relieved that apparently I wasn't going to be raped today. Or murdered.

"It really is." Parker gripped my nipple between his thumb and forefinger and squeezed.

I winced.

Hunter moved so his face was right in front of mine, close enough for his breath to brush my cheek.

"We are reasonable, you know," he said as though that was actually true. "Reuben doesn't expect Zeke to quit the band in the middle of the tour. All he has to do is assure our big brother that he'll come back to the family when it's over. Otherwise, we will find you again. Next time, we'll make sure we have longer to play with you. A few days maybe."

The idea made me want to bring up my break-fast. And last night's dinner.

"What would your girlfriend think of that?" I asked.

Hunter froze in surprise. He forced a smile onto his face, obviously trying to cover the fact I'd caught him off guard. "What girlfriend would that be?"

I wasn't sure if I should step in any deeper or back the fuck off right now, but I doubted he was going to let it go until I told him what I knew.

"Lila Bell," I said.

According to Asher's brother Dane, the Brantley twins were sleeping with her. From what Dane said, Reuben would be pissed if he knew. Zeke wrestled with the idea of telling him. Judging by Hunter's reaction, he hadn't, and neither had anyone else. He was probably working under the illusion no one knew.

Surprise, asshole. Only, how fucked was I for springing it on him?

Hunter's eyes flicked to Parker. He looked more than slightly alarmed. That sent a shiver of fear through me. This could either be a bargaining chip, or my death warrant.

"It's interesting you know that," Parker said slowly. He moved into view and sat down beside me.

"Does Reuben know?" I asked. Fuck it, I'd gone this far, I might as well wade right on in. When neither of them answered, I continued. "Would you prefer he not know? Because Zeke knows. He might be persuaded to keep his mouth shut."

"It's not that simple." Hunter looked discon-certed for the first time since he'd taken my blindfold off. "We're only here doing what Reuben told us to do."

"Kidnap me and threatened me with rape?" I said. "Your brother is charming. Not."

Hunter shrugged. "Whatever it takes to get his way."

"What will he do with you if he hears you're fucking Lila?" I asked.

They exchanged glances again. "We'd prefer he didn't know about it just yet," Parker said.

"In return for what?" I wanted them to promise to leave me, Zeke and the rest of the guys alone if we kept our mouths shut, but that didn't seem to be in their power to give. If Reuben sent them somewhere, they would go, or risk whatever punishment he would give them if they refused. I suspected that wouldn't be pretty. Not that I gave a shit about that, but it was what it was.

"We'll go back to Reuben and tell him you're working on Zeke," Hunter said. "That's all we can offer."

"How about you promise not to rape me, no matter what Reuben asks you to do," I said. "We can always pretend you did." Was I really having this conversation? Yes, for fuck sake I was. Self preservation was important to me.

Hunter sighed like he was giving up his left arm. "Fine, we promise. But I can't promise Reuben won't send somebody else."

"Noted," I said. "Now you can tell me how long I've been here and if I've missed the concert?"

"Only a couple of hours," Parker said. "I guess we could drop you off at the venue before we fly back to Sydney."

How fucking big of them. At least I believed them when they made their promise.

Of course, that didn't mean they wouldn't kill me.

11

TULLY

"WHAT THE FUCK, DUDE?" I muttered under my breath. "We shouldn't be here."

"I know, but we have to," Zeke said, every bit as frustrated as I was. "The show must go fucking on."

I opened my mouth to respond, but bit back my anger. It was nothing we hadn't said over and over the last few hours. Abbie was out there and we were supposed to pretend everything was fine and get on with the concert?

Things weren't fine.

Things were fucked the fuck fucking up.

"If it wasn't for Penn and his big, fucking mouth." Asher glared daggers at Penn, who rolled his eyes in response.

"I didn't make the silly bitch walk out," the keyboardist retorted.

I put a hand on Asher's arm before he threw himself at Penn and punched his lights out.

Honestly, it stopped me from doing the same thing.

"Jackson is out there doing what he can to find her," Landon said. "Along with everyone the tour can spare."

"We should be out there," Landon said sulkily. "If it was any one of us, we would be."

"Landon is right," Asher said. "If one of us was missing, the rest of us would be out there looking." He glanced at Penn like he was thinking he might not bother if the keyboardist went missing.

Penn flipped him off. "Chances are, she'll come crawling back any minute now, and all of this worry was for nothing. She probably put down her phone and then fucking forgot when she put it. She's been out there all this time looking for it."

I considered the possibility she put her phone down and walked off without realising, but if that was the case, she would have returned to the hotel hours ago. Or made her way here, to the stadium.

It wasn't far from the hotel... if she was capable of walking here.

At this point, the only thing that made sense was the one thing none of us wanted to think about.

Someone took her. The only, and preferable, alternative was that she was so pissed off at all of us, she deliberately stayed away. I knew what happened brought back memories for her, but I didn't think she was so furious she would hide for hours, or miss the concert.

I was about to lower my hand from Asher's arm, but I slipped it over his shoulders instead.

"She'll be okay," I said firmly. "She's strong and tough. The world has thrown a shit load of things at her and it hasn't broken her. She was angry, but she'll get over it."

He looked miserable, but he nodded. "I wish we hadn't agreed to that stupid publicity shit. If we hadn't done that, she would be here, getting ready to go on stage." He glanced towards the hydraulics for the steps which led up to the stage.

They were currently closed while Blazing Violet performed. The support act had just started, so there was still time for Abbie to appear.

I sent a plea to the universe to make it happen. We hadn't waited millions of years to meet, only to have it end so quickly.

"No offence, dude, but I wish you hadn't too. Or

at least told her or me what the fuck was going on. But it's done now and can't be undone. We have to move on from it." Which would only be possible after Abbie returned to us.

I had to believe it was a when and not an if.

"I'm coming to the conclusion the rest of them can't be left unsupervised without you, Tull," Penn said dryly.

"No shit," I said. "I'm away from you guys one night and all hell breaks loose."

"The moral of the story is, don't go off by yourself," Penn said.

"Fuck that." The night Abbie and I shared was one I would never forget. I planned on a repeat performance as soon as we could find a time and place.

After all, she wasn't pissed off at me. Although, she would be if I admitted I would have done the same thing the other guys did. And honestly, I would tell her. I hated keeping secrets from people I cared about. If it meant she punched me in the cock, then so be it.

Better yet, she could save it until we were alone and paddle my ass as hard as she wanted. Okay, first of all, I didn't need to be alone for that, and second of all, I would enjoy it. It might make her feel better though. As far as I was concerned, everybody won.

I paced from the hydraulic stairs to the door of the green room and back again.

While I did that, I ran through the events of this morning through my head. What could we have done differently? We could have used the tracker sooner. We could have gagged Penn. I could have kept her in bed for a few more hours until she was too exhausted to be angry.

Okay, I wouldn't get away with the last one. I managed to distract her for a little while, but she had to deal with those photos at some point. Maybe I should have tied her up and gone to yell at the guys before she could?

Everything seemed to be one long *maybe if...* which at the end of the day changed absolutely nothing. Abbie wasn't here and we were going to have to go onstage and explain her absence. Or not explain and hope the audience didn't throw things at us.

Either way, I wasn't looking forward to performing tonight.

"I'm going to call Jackson," Zeke said impatiently. "He must know something by now."

I didn't bother to correct him. We all knew if Jackson found her, he would have called one of us. Whatever, if it made Zeke feel better, there was no harm in trying.

He moved away from the stairs, to a quieter part of the backstage area and put the phone to his ear.

It was clear he didn't like what he heard. He looked like he was going to turn and walk out of the stadium before our set even began.

I walked over to him as he mashed his thumb against the screen to end the call and shoved his phone forcefully into the back of his jeans.

"Still nothing?" I asked.

"Not a thing," he growled. "It seems like no one has seen her. It's like she dropped off the face of the fucking earth."

That did nothing to settle my anxiety for the woman. If the audience wouldn't notice, I'd leave the stadium and go looking for her. I was sorely tempted. Being here seemed all kinds of wrong. The woman we all cared about was fuck knows where and we were supposed to go out there and pretend we were having the time of our lives.

Surely concerts were cancelled for lesser reasons?

I scrubbed my face with my hand and shook my head. "This is bullshit. Blazing Violet will be finished soon. What the fuck are we supposed to do?"

"Abbie," Asher said.

"Well of course we'd all like to do Abbie—"

"No, Abbie," Asher insisted. He gestured behind me.

I turned around to see her hurrying up the corridor. She looked pale and tired, but in one, beautiful, glorious piece.

We all started toward her, but I was the first one to reach her, put my arms around her and pick her up off her feet. "Where the fuck have you been?"

She gave a little squeal and I set her down. "It's a long story. I'm sorry I'm late."

"Late?" Asher echoed. "You've been missing for hours and we've been worried sick, and you're concerned about being late?" He all but shoved me aside and gave her a firm hug.

"Like I said, it's a long story." She hugged him back. "I'll tell you about it later. It sounds like it's almost my turn to go on."

"It is," Zeke agreed. He had his phone to his ear again. "Yes, she turned up. She's here at the stadium. No, she's fine." He listened for a moment, then shook his head. "No, we don't know where she's been, but you should get your ass here. Yep, bye."

He gave her a hug and said, "Jackson and a bunch of others were out there looking for you. Are you all right?"

"I'm fine," she said lightly.

She didn't seem fine to me, but I suspected that was all we were going to get out of her for now.

"You worried the shit out of me." Zeke pressed his mouth to hers in a hard, heated kiss.

"She worried the shit out of all of us." I eyed Penn. If he said anything stupid now, I might do something I'd regret. Like push him off the stage in front of fifty thousand people. Or grab one of Asher's drumsticks and shove it up his ass.

Whatever it was, I'd probably have to get in line to do it.

"Abbie!" Landon and Channing came bounding down the corridor from the green room like a pair of golden retrievers. When Zeke stepped back, they both threw their arms around her.

She hugged them both back. "I'm sorry for scaring you and I'm sorry for overreacting." She, too, eyed Penn as though expecting him to say something shitty.

For once, he had the sense to keep his mouth shut.

I still might shove him off the stage.

"This is Blazing Violet's last song," Zeke said. "Are you really up to going out there?" He put his hands on her shoulders and leaned her back to look her in the face.

"Yeah, I'm fine," she said. "If I'm not going to let a little can in the face stop me, then I'm not going to let being late stop me either. I'll be okay. I promise."

"Promise never to run off like that again," Zeke insisted. "There's a killer out there. Did you forget that?" The only time he had that soft look on his face was when he looked at Asher. Clearly his feelings for both of them ran deep.

She gave him a watery smile. "For a couple of minutes, I did. Look, I can't explain it now. After the concert I will tell you everything. I swear."

I knew I wasn't the only one getting the vibe that something bad happened to her. I also knew she wasn't going to tell us until she was ready. Whatever it was, she wasn't going to let it get in the way of tonight's performance. Did that mean it was only something minor that didn't matter, or something so bad it would distract all of us?

Either way, I was going to have half my mind on her and the other half on the concert. I didn't know when she had become more important to me than music, but she had.

I was one hundred percent here for it.

12

ABBIE

"I'm GOING to kill those motherfucking pricks," Zeke snarled. "They fucking took you in broad daylight and threatened you?"

"Yeah." That and more. I didn't want to tell him the evil twins got touchy with me. I managed a quick shower after they dropped me off at the hotel, but my skin still crawled. Thinking about the way they touched me was bad enough. Talking about it…

At some point, maybe I'd be ready to share more details. For now, I kept it vague.

I had a feeling the guys knew what I wasn't telling them anyway.

"For what it's worth, I threatened them back," I said. "It would seem Reuben still doesn't know about their relationship with Lila Bell. And they'd like it to stay that way. They agreed to give us some breathing space in return for us keeping our mouths shut."

"You blackmailed the Brantley twins?" Tully seemed impressed.

Asher groaned. "It's not gonna take them very long to realise where you got that information from."

I glanced at him regretfully. "Dane. I didn't mean to bring your brother into it. I freaked out and spoke without thinking."

It wasn't until an hour or two later I realised what I'd said and the trouble my big mouth might have caused.

Asher spread his hands out to either side, palms upward. "Dane can take care of himself. I should tell him they know. Although, they won't go after him now. If they did, Reuben would want to know why. I'm sure he'll find some way to turn all of this to his advantage. Dane is nothing if not an opportunist."

I rubbed my wrists where the restraints left bruises. "They said they didn't kill any of the victims. I have to say I believed them. They'd brag about it, wouldn't they?"

"Yeah," Zeke agreed. "That doesn't mean Reuben didn't send someone else. He has a phonebook of assassins to call on."

He glanced toward Tully. "I know it doesn't look like a professional did it, but that might be what he wants us to think. Fuck only knows what goes through his head."

Tully conceded the point with a nod. "It's possible the kills look rough on purpose."

"What do you mean rough?" Channing asked. He and Landon were sitting side-by-side on the couch, sipping beer and eating pizza.

I only managed a slice or two before my stomach rebelled. Whatever the twins drugged me with was still affecting my system. Or my nerves were. Either way, the food wasn't sitting well.

"A professional would use a more precise incision to remove the—" Tully started.

I interrupted him. "Do we have to talk about that now? Some of you are eating and, personally, I'm trying to hold down what I already have." I grimaced and swallowed hard.

"Yeah, sorry." Tully picked up his beer from the table in front of him and moved over to sit next to me on the end of the bed. "No more gross stuff for today."

When he placed an arm around me, I nestled against him. "Thank you."

My eyes went over to Penn, who sat in the chair

in the corner, quietly sipping beer. He hadn't said a word for the last couple of hours.

If I didn't know better, I'd think he felt bad for the things he said. Not because he didn't mean them, but because of what happened after. It wasn't entirely his fault, but fucked if I was going to tell him that. I was too tired to be pissed off at him, but I might resume being angry at him later.

"Speaking of gross stuff," Zeke started, "you were right about those photos. They were supposed to introduce Cameo Orchid to new fans, but that's wasn't the way to do it. I, for one, promise shit like that won't happen again."

The other guys muttered their agreement.

I managed a faint smile in response. "It better not," I growled, more playful than firm, or angry.

The whole thing with the photo seemed like such a small deal now. It was just a photo for publicity. At the end of the day, the music industry was a business like any other. Crap like this was all too common. I needed to put it in the, 'shit happens,' box and move on.

"I can't believe you went out on stage and sang after what they did," Asher said. "Everyone would have understood if you'd been too freaked out to perform."

He gave me a soft look that conveyed so much emotion. He was a big, badass, muscular rock god on the outside, but a soft, sweet, squishy marshmallow on the inside. I adored him for it.

I shrugged. "I guess I'm a badass after all. Besides, the audience wouldn't have understood."

That was another act of pretence. That everything was absolutely fine in my world. That was exactly why I didn't tell the guys what happened before they went out on stage. Zeke's reaction said it all. He would have been too busy being angry and wanting to rip his brothers' heads off to go out and have a good time. As it was, he held back for the first song or two before he found his groove.

I knew he was worried about me, but all I would have done was make it worse.

"We would have told them you were sick," Zeke said reasonably. "It happens all the time. Last-minute food poisoning or laryngitis. No one would question either of those."

"Unless she started speaking," Asher pointed out.

Zeke punched him lightly on the arm. "You know what I mean, dickhead. We tell them whatever. What are they going to do? Tell us we're lying? They won't do shit."

"Food poisoning would have been plausible,

given the way I'm feeling, Whatever they gave me..."
I shook my head and grimaced.

"Should we take you to the hospital?" Tully looked worried. "If they gave you something nasty, it might have a lasting impact."

I waved him off. "I'm fine. Nothing a good night's sleep wouldn't fix." I hoped, because doctors asked questions and I didn't want to have to give them any answers. Bruises on my wrists and ankles would be difficult to explain.

Not to mention the ones on my ass from Tully's paddle.

"You said they were flying back to Sydney?" Zeke asked.

"That's what they said," I agreed. Who knew if it was true? They weren't exactly fine, upstanding citizens.

"I'll look into it and see," he said. "I want to make sure that's where they actually went. Those two are like a pair of snakes, slithering around and popping up when they're not wanted. Which is most of the fucking time. If we weren't leaving the country in a couple of days, I'd follow them and tear them both a new one."

"I'd go with you," Asher said.

"Me too," Tully agreed.

"And us," Landon said.

Channing nodded in agreement. Not that he needed to. Wherever Landon went, he went.

I wondered if they ever disagreed about anything. They must, but I'd never heard it. Not yet anyway.

My gaze returned to Penn.

He looked back at me, something dark in his eyes. "I'm always up for ripping the heads off little motherfuckers," he growled. "Kidnapping helpless women is a dog act. They deserve to have their balls served to them on a plate."

I wasn't sure how I felt about being referred to as helpless but I couldn't argue with the rest of it.

"Yeah, they do," Zeke said. "At some point I'm going to have to deal with them. They need to back the fuck off. I'm done with this bullshit. Furthermore," he looked at me firmly, "if you ever go off alone like that again, it won't just be Tully paddling your ass. We can't keep you safe if you do things like that."

I sighed. "I know. Although, a girl should be able to walk around by herself without getting kidnapped." Since they already did it to me twice, I had to agree that not being alone was a good idea.

"Yes, you should," he said. "But no going off by

yourself, at least until we know it's safe out there. We need to figure out who is killing people, and get all my brothers to fuck off. Even after that…"

"I'm going to have one of you following me around for the rest of my life?" I asked. I could think of worse ways to spend my time, but it was going to get really old for them fast. Wasn't it?

"You want the answer to that?" Zeke rubbed a hand over the back of his head.

He seemed like he was worried I wanted clarification that he was prepared to make a lifetime commitment.

I wasn't ready for that, not yet. We had plenty of time.

"The answer is yes," Asher said with certainty. "Maybe I'll quit the band and become your bodyguard." He looked like he was actually considering it.

"That might be a bit extreme," I said.

"No shit," Penn muttered. "We can multitask."

"We?" Asher swivelled around to face him.

Penn grunted. "She's not going away anytime soon, is she? If I don't help in some way, it will piss you guys off."

"So you will do it so you don't piss us off," Tully said slowly. "Is that the only reason?"

Every eye in the room was on Penn now.

He narrowed his eyes and looked like an angry, cornered animal. "Has anyone told you guys peer pressure is lame?"

"He's right," Zeke said. "He'll admit it when he's ready."

Penn rolled his eyes toward the ceiling. "Give it a fucking rest."

"Only when you—" Asher started.

Penn interrupted him by picking up an olive off his pizza and flicking it at Asher. It hit the drummer on the cheek and bounced off his face.

"What the fuck?" Asher glared at him. "Why do people keep throwing food at me?"

"Because you deserve it." Penn threw a chunk of pineapple in his direction.

Asher caught it and ate it. He grimaced. "Shit, I forgot I hate pineapple."

We all laughed, including him.

"You guys suck," he said with a grin. He stuck out his tongue with distaste.

"That's what you like about us," Zeke said. "We suck, and taste better than pineapple."

"That's what I like about you and Abbie," Asher agreed. "The rest of them, not so much. I'm a one man and woman guy."

Zeke leaned over to give Asher a kiss so hot I

forgot how tired I was.

These guys, they knew how to get me going without trying. The whole day was pushed out of my head. All I could think about now was watching them, and the way Tully felt with his arm around me.

"Get a room," Penn said.

"This is our room," Asher said. "If you don't want to watch, feel free to go somewhere else." To punctuate his words, he wound his arms around Zeke's neck and pulled him closer, until the singer was almost lying on top of him on the other bed.

"Fucking hell," Penn muttered. "I need more beer." He stood and grabbed another bottle from the fridge, but didn't leave.

"I guess that means he wants to watch," Tully said.

"I guess so." I slid my arms around Tully's neck and drew him to me.

"You don't mind an audience?" Landon asked. "Because I'd like to stay too, if that's okay?"

"Me too," Channing agreed.

"Fine by me," I said.

Tully didn't say anything, but judging by the way he pushed me back on the bed gently and laid his weight full-length on top of me, he didn't object either.

Zeke and Asher were busy tearing off each other's clothes. I wasn't sure if they even heard. Presumably, on some level, they were aware of the other guys' presence in the room.

I caught a glimpse of Channing and Landon kissing on the couch and almost felt sorry for Penn, who sat by himself. At least he had his hand. Hell, if he wanted to join in, he'd be welcome. Did he realise that?

As Tully and I started to remove each other's clothes, I forgot to worry about it. All I knew was the way the air touched my skin when Tully peeled off my skirt and blouse.

I closed my eyes and let myself slip back into the place I was in last night, where all I did was feel, smell and taste.

Thankfully, Tully didn't suggest putting the blindfold on me again. Either it didn't occur to him or he thought it might freak me out after what the evil twins did. Ruining that for me was further confirmation they were evil.

"Can I take off your bra and panties?" Tully whispered in my ear. "Do you mind the other guys seeing you?"

"No," I said without thinking. "I mean, yes. You

can take them off, I don't mind." I opened my eyes to see him smile before I closed them again.

I wanted them to see me. All of me. I felt less vulnerable naked with these six guys than I did fully dressed around the twins, or even onstage. And a whole lot sexier.

I rolled over onto my stomach so he could unhook my bra, then rolled back so he could slide it off. Then my panties.

"Holy shit," someone muttered. It sounded like Penn.

Knowing he was watching made me wetter than the Murray River during a downpour. Added to that was the sounds of the other guys making out and my senses were going wild.

Asher groaned.

I opened my eyes and glanced over. I was glad I did.

Zeke was propped on one elbow, his mouth around Asher's cock. He looked over at me and smiled around his delicious mouthful.

I smiled back. I knew he didn't want to rush things, being new to having sex with another guy and all. Going down on Asher was a huge step for him and I was here to see it.

And it was fucking hot.

I glanced over to the couch where Landon and Channing were lying top to tail, cocks in each other's mouths.

Holy hotness.

"There seems to be a trend here," I said to Tully as he slipped off his T-shirt.

"I noticed that." He dropped his shirt on the floor.

"I'd hate to be off trend." I sat up and pushed him back before lying beside him and undoing his jeans. "Can I take off the rest of your clothes?"

He laced his hands behind his head, the picture of a confident rock god. "You absolutely can."

Did he have any idea how sexy he was?

"Thank you," I said graciously. I slid down his jeans and smiled at his boxers, which were decorated with smiley face emojis. Very badass. They soon joined my clothes on the floor.

I curled my hand around the base of his cock and worked my fingers up and down, making him rock hard and throbbing hot. I closed my eyes again and massaged his balls until a groan washed from him. I hooked my hand over his slit to feel his pre-cum before I tasted it with the tip of my tongue.

Delicious.

Before I could lower my mouth onto him, he

swivelled around and pulled me over to straddle his face. He blew a warm breath onto my pussy.

"Now here's one hell of a view," he said happily.

"It looks pretty good from here too." I shivered with delight before lowering my mouth onto his cock and starting to suck.

He gripped my hips with his fingers and traced slow, tantalising circles around my clit and into my folds. The harder he lapped, the harder I sucked.

The whole world disappeared, leaving only the taste of him and the way he filled my mouth, the wet sounds of sucking and groans from all around the room. Both mine and from all the other guys.

I opened my eyes and glanced over to Penn. It was worth it to see the concentration on his face, and the way he was looking at me. We locked eyes on each other and, as pissed off as I still was with him, I couldn't help myself. I came, rolling my hips and grinding my pussy against Tully's mouth.

Penn, being the fucker he was, grinned, clearly taking credit for my orgasm.

Yeah, okay, whatever. I was quickly too busy with Tully coming, and keeping rhythm with him.

He gasped, "Can I come in your mouth?"

"Mmmhmm, I said in agreement, my mouth too

full for words. Fuller still when he came, hot juices flooding my throat.

My eyes still on Penn, I swallowed down every drop.

His eyes widened and he came, bucking into his hand and spilling pearly cum over his fingers.

I slid my mouth off Tully's cock and grinned. Now it was my turn to take credit for his orgasm.

Penn made a face at me, but at least he didn't flip me off. Although, he was kinda busy pulling his track pants back into place before he headed to the bathroom to wash his hand.

He couldn't deny I did it for him.

The feeling was mutual. One of these days...

13

ABBIE

"I THOUGHT YOU MIGHT NEED THIS." Zeke reached into his suitcase and pulled out something.

"How did you have my phone?" I took it from him and looked it over. It didn't have any damage, as far as I could see. Thank fuck for that. My bank account was still not healthy enough to afford a new phone. Honestly, every dollar the label gave me so far had gone on outstanding bills.

I don't mean outstanding in the good way. I came painfully close to having to declare bankruptcy. If it wasn't for Levi Jones, I would have been screwed.

"We found it on a bench in the park," Zeke said. "I presume that was when you bumped into my dear brothers." Apparently a night of fucking and sleep hadn't dimmed his anger.

"Yes, it was." I tried to suppress a shudder but failed. Every time I thought about yesterday, my stomach twisted and my whole body wanted to freeze up. I guessed this was why Zeke wanted me to learn how to use a gun. If I froze with a weapon in my hand, things wouldn't end well. An assailant might take it and use it on me.

"Can you guys teach me self-defence?" I asked. "Realistically, you can't watch me twenty-four hours a day, seven days a week."

"Yes, we can. Even if we have to take turns having a shower with you." He smiled.

"What a chore," I said ironically. "Am I still allowed to go to the toilet by myself?"

"I want to say no, but I have a feeling you would punch me in the face if I did." He leaned his upper body back as if he was actually scared of that possibility.

"I wouldn't punch you in the face," I told him. "I'd hurt my hand. I can't rule out throwing things at you though."

He chuckled. "Maybe we shouldn't teach you self-defence. You might use it against me." He raised his arm in front of his face.

"I think you're confusing defence with offence," I said. "I wouldn't mind learning how to throw a few kicks and punches. It's got to be better than receiving them."

He put his arms around me and drew me to him until my face rested against his chest. "If I have it my way, no one will throw punches, or anything else, at you. Not physically or verbally. They sure as fuck won't be drugging you and dragging you away again."

"I too have a preference for me not being drugged and dragged away," I said. "Being that vulnerable is…" I shook my head. "It was scary as hell." They could have done literally anything to me, and I would have been powerless to stop them.

A tiny voice in the back of my mind asked if maybe they did something while I was asleep. I silenced that fucker. If they had, I'd be sore and sticky when I woke, and I was neither.

He stroked my hair. "Did…" He started hesitantly. "Did they do anything other than what you've told me already?" He pulled back and looked me in the eyes. Worry lived in his, laced with that still-simmering fury.

I knew what he was asking, but I was scared to put it into words. My tongue darted over my lips.

"They touched me a little bit," I said finally. "Nothing that went too far but—"

"Fuck," Zeke growled. "I will rip off their nuts and shove them down their throats."

"As much as I'd like to see that, I made them promise not to...you know, rape me, if we didn't tell Reuben about Lila Bell." I couldn't meet his gaze now. Couldn't deal with his anger. My own emotions were overwhelming enough.

"How the *hell* did you have that conversation?" he barked.

I hesitated. "They implied they would force themselves on me the next time they came for me, if you don't listen to what Reuben wants."

If I thought Zeke was angry before, it was nothing compared to now. His face turned red. I wouldn't have been surprised to see steam pouring out of his ears.

I actually flinched.

"They threatened to rape you if I don't do what Reuben says?" His tone would have been terrifying if it was directed at me.

I had no doubt if Hunter and Parker were in front of him right now, he would literally kill them. Reuben too.

"Yeah, but now they won't, because you'll tell Reuben about Lila. They're so shit scared about him finding out, we have them by the balls, so to speak."

My tone was lighter than I felt. It was all very well until the day Reuben found out and we lost our leverage. What would happen then? Presumably all bets would be off.

"Those little pricks," Zeke growled. "If I'd known they would grow up to be monsters, I would have drowned them in the bath when they were babies."

I put a hand on his cheek, felt the roughness of his stubble under my fingertips.

"You never would have done that," I said. "You're not a monster, you just have some nasty relatives. Who we will deal with, because we are big, badass rock gods."

He looked surprised but managed a faint smile. "That's the first time I've heard you refer to yourself as a rock god."

I shrugged. "Yeah, well, I'm more of a rock princess, but close enough."

"You're a female alpha wolf," he said. "Complete with the teeth to rip the throat out of your enemies."

"I don't know about that, but I like the sound of it," I said. "Abbie the alpha wolf."

"Mate to Zeke, also the alpha wolf." He pulled me back to him and nuzzled his face into my hair. "And the rest of the crazy wolf pack. We're all ready to tear out the throats of your enemies. I'll start with my brothers."

"Do you think Hunter and Parker would be different if it wasn't for Reuben's influence?" I asked.

"Would they not be dickheads if they were left to think for themselves? I have no idea," he admitted. "I'm sure they'd find some other shit to get into. If they get involved with the Bell family, then they'll have a whole different set of influences. Worse ones than Reuben, if that's possible."

I didn't much like the sound of that.

I leaned against him and listened to the comforting beat of his heart for a couple of minutes. "How did you know where to find my phone?"

He stiffened.

I pulled back and looked up at him. "Zeke?"

His expression made me think it was more than just a lucky guess.

"What did you do?" Whatever it was, it had him looking guilty as shit. For some reason, my mind went straight to thinking maybe he was in on the kidnapping with his brothers.

Yeah, okay, that was stupid, but that was where my mind went. I actually started to feel everything crumbling down around me.

He must have seen that on my face, because he quickly said, "I put a tracker on your phone."

"Oh." I couldn't decide if that was better, worse, or just as bad. Honestly, it took a full minute to process what he said.

"Wait a minute, you put a fucking tracker on my phone? Without my knowledge or consent? In what world is it okay to put a tracker on your girlfriend's phone and not mention it?"

"In the world where there's a motherfucking murderer and a mobster after us both," he said calm and reasonable. "And we have no idea if they are the same person or two different people. I told you I would do whatever I had to do to keep you safe. This was one thing I could do that should have fucking helped, but it fucking didn't. I failed to protect you. I will not fail at that again. If I have to give up the band, if I have to give up everything, I will protect the woman I love."

"Love?" I echoed. Was that just a word he threw out there in the heat of the moment?

He bent to touch his forehead to mine. "Yes, love. I love you, Abbie."

My heart raced faster than one of those high speed trains in Japan. Tears sprang to my eyes, then slid down my cheeks.

He brushed them away with his thumb. "I'm sorry, I didn't mean to upset you." My response seemed to have him genuinely confused.

I shook my head slightly. "You didn't upset me. I love you too, Zeke Brantley. Even with your crazy family and all the shit that's gone on. I don't regret a moment I've spent with you. From the very second I saw you in that club." That felt like years ago now. Decades. A lifetime.

He breathed a sigh of relief. "That's good, because it would have been as awkward as fuck if you said you hate my guts or something."

I slapped him lightly on the chest and laughed. "I could never hate your guts."

"Even when strange women sit on my lap for publicity photos?" He looked tentative and unsure if he should have brought that up or not.

"Even then," I said. "I can be pissed off once in a while, that doesn't mean I would stop loving you. I'm sure you'll find plenty to get pissed off at me about."

"Never," he said firmly. "Worried, anxious, nervous, but never angry or pissed off. Unless you start snoring really loud. Or say Violet is a better lead singer than I am. Or tell me all the guys have bigger cocks than I do."

I shook my head at him and laughed. "I have no

control over whether or not I snore, but I would never say the rest of it. Even if it was true."

He raised an eyebrow.

"Which it's not," I said to put him out of his misery.

He wiped the back of his hand across his brow. "Phew. You had me worried for a moment there. I mean, not really; I know I am pretty fucking amazing and have a massive cock."

"It matches your massive ego," I teased.

"My ego and my cock are a match made in heaven," he said. "Just like you and I." He kissed me lightly.

I kissed him back and then asked, "Do I have to worry about having a tracker anywhere else? There's not one on me somewhere is there?" I started to pat myself down as if I would find one that way.

He chuckled. "No, just your phone. Now you mention it, I should put one in your watch. And one of your earrings." He cocked his head and looked at my ears. "Anything you would have to take out to go through airport security, or that they wouldn't worry about because it's already metal."

"Don't you dare," I growled. "It's bad enough you put one on my phone. I don't need you tracing me every second of every day." I lightly rested a hand on his chest. "I appreciate you wanting to take care of me, but that would be excessive. Okay?" Not to mention what might happen if the tracker was hacked. The last thing I needed was anyone else in his family knowing where I was and what I was doing. Or the killer. Or the press, for that matter. Rather than keep me safe, it might make me a target.

Hard pass.

"Do you have a tracker in your phone?" His hesitation to respond told me everything I needed to know. "Maybe you should. What happens if you go missing?"

"Anyone who tried anything with me would have a very short life expectancy," he said. "But if it'll make you feel better, I'll put one in my phone. And all the other guys' too."

"I'm not sure if it would make me feel better, but if you think it will keep us all safer, then do it," I said. If it was good enough for me, then it was good enough for everyone else.

"I think I hear the guys back with breakfast," Zeke said.

"It's about time." I was actually starting to get hungry. For food.

ABBIE

"HOLY SHIT." Violet's eyes were huge. "Jackson said you had some trouble with Zeke's brothers. Something about you being kidnapped?" She looked as though she wouldn't believe it until she heard it from me.

She drew me a little apart from the guys. Zeke looked like he was about to argue, but I waved him back. What was going to happen here, in full view of everyone?

He nodded, but pointed to his eyes, then my face. He was watching closely. Got it.

I blew him a kiss and followed Violet. Evidently, knowledge of Zeke's family went beyond the band and the manager. Who else knew about them? It was starting to feel like the worst kept secret in Australia. An exaggeration, no doubt.

Maybe.

"So, is it true?" she pressed. She looked very much like she wanted me to deny it.

I shrugged. "Something like that, yeah. I'm okay though. It was no big deal."

She narrowed her eyes at me sceptically. "No big deal? *Right*, because people get kidnapped every day."

It was starting to feel that way, yes.

Hopefully they weren't planning to make a habit of it. There were better ways to spend my day than being drugged and tied up.

Like being tied up and spanked.

Before I could answer, one of the tour staff hurried past, carrying a large box.

I stepped over closer to the wall to get out of their way. I couldn't help eyeing the box as he carried it down the corridor toward the door. Chances were, it contained something completely innocent, like empty water bottles.

I shook my head. I was getting paranoid. There were probably no body parts in that box. Part of me wanted to chase the guy down and check.

That wouldn't look suspicious as fuck would it?

Since it would, I cleared my throat, leaned back against the wall and tried to look as casual as I could.

"Lucky for me, they just wanted to talk," I said evenly. "They just have a... a slightly heavy-handed way of going about it."

That was an exaggeration. For all I knew, Reuben told them to talk to me, and they decided on the method themselves. Since they were both the evil twin, they'd gone with sneaking up behind me and drugging me.

Whatever shit they'd used to knock me out seemed to be out of my system now. Hopefully without leaving any lasting damage. If it did, I might join the guys in tracking down the twins to feed their own balls to them.

Hell, I might do that anyway.

"Just a little, from what Jackson said," Violet agreed. "What the fuck happened? You're always surrounded by six hulking rock stars. Did they jump you while you were in the toilet or something?"

I sighed. Since she apparently wasn't going to let it go, I pushed myself off the wall and waved towards a side room. It was out of sight of any of the guys, but I should be safe in there with Violet. In the unlikely event she tried something, I only had to shout and they would come running.

Just in case, I left the door ajar.

The room looked like an office of some kind, with a couple of desks on either wall. I sat on one of them and crossed my legs. I told her about the photo and how I got angry with the guys and stormed off. I expected her to laugh or think the way Penn had, that I overreacted.

Instead, she nodded her understanding. "I've met most of Cameo Orchid. They're lovely, but they would one hundred percent jump the guys' bones, given half a chance. Those photos for sure have that vibe. As for the guys... Until you came along, they would have totally gone there. Without a second thought. But you know what?" She reached out and put a hand on my arm. "Next time they piss you off, come and talk to me. We can have a good, old-fashioned bitch session about them. With optional ice cream."

I smiled. "Bitch sessions are one of my top three favourite kinds of sessions."

She grinned and together we said, "After sex sessions and jam sessions." We both fell into laughter.

"See?" she said once she had regained her composure. "It's good to have another woman around. We're surrounded by so much testosterone, it's easy

MAGGIE ALABASTER

to forget we have options. For the record, I'm not complaining about all that testosterone, but variety is the spice of life."

"So they say," I agreed. "It's just...I'm not used to having female friends."

Candy, the producer, and I got along really well. And now Violet and I, but I wasn't used to confiding in another woman. Or... much of anyone really. I used to tell Vance everything and look where that got me.

"You better start getting used to it," Violet said. "Because you're stuck with me for the next couple of months." She popped out her hip and planted her fist on it, as though daring me to contradict her.

After a moment, she relaxed her pose. "Don't get me wrong, we don't have to be friends and you don't have to tell me anything. But I like you and I think sometimes it's good to have a break from all those guys. You know? I know I need a break from mine. Especially Blaise." She rolled her eyes towards the ceiling.

"He seems like a handful," I said.

She snorted a laugh. "He certainly is that. In more ways than one, I'm guessing. I wouldn't know, since we haven't gone there, if you know what I mean?"

"Yeah, I know what you mean." I guessed that

about them. They seem to have the same kind of relationship Penn and I have; antagonistic but with a hint of lust. Okay, more than a hint, but we still wanted to strangle each other more than we wanted to fuck each other.

For now.

"We should go out for a drink sometime," she suggested. "If the guys will let you out of their sight for long enough."

I laughed bitterly. "I'd love to go out for a drink, but they'd probably surround us like circling wagons, to make sure we're safe."

"As long as they don't interfere, then I'm down for that." She sat on the other desk. "You've been through some shit, haven't you?"

"That's an understatement." I sighed. "I seem to be a magnet for it. Maybe I was a total asshole in a past life. I mean, that would explain it, wouldn't it?"

"Nah, I can't imagine you being an asshole, even in a past life." She waved her hand in a gesture of dismissal. "In my experience, it all comes down to jealousy."

"That was what Tully said." I placed my hands to either side of me on the desktop and leaned back slightly.

"Tully can be a wise dude when he wants to be,"

she said. "People see successful women and love to tear us down. I don't only mean stale, pale males. Some women are just as bad. Worse. Especially if they think we're after their man or some shit."

"Like me being angry over those photos?" Looking back, I felt shitty about the whole thing and the way I reacted. Not just because of the kidnapping, but because I didn't want to be that kind of woman. The one who tries to pussywhip men.

She tilted her head. "You were pissed off at the guys, not the girls. Right? I bet it never occurred to you to try to tear them down or go after them."

"No, it didn't," I admitted. "When the guys said it was the women who suggested sitting on their laps, I was still pissed off at the guys for doing it."

"Why was that?" Violet asked curiously. "Why not be angry at the girls for suggesting it?"

I thought about that for a moment. "I don't know. Is it arrogant as shit to say I didn't see them as a threat? If the guys did anything, it would be them betraying our relationship, not those women. I mean, if it wasn't them, it would have been someone else."

"Plenty of girls would blame the other woman for seducing their man," Violet said.

I snorted. "That's such bullshit. You can't seduce someone unless they want to be seduced."

Violet snapped her fingers loud enough to make me jump. "Exactly. You should hang out with the Orchid girls sometime. They're sweet and super talented, but naïve as fuck. They could use some big sisters like us. Girls who have been around and have seen enough to know the pitfalls of this industry. Mind you, they made the right choice signing with White Wolf Records. They have plenty of us looking out for them."

"I wish I had us a year or two ago," I said with a sigh. "It would have been nice to have someone kick my ass in the right direction. And save me from making stupid mistakes like marrying Vance."

"Would a kick have helped?" Violet tilted her head so her purple ponytail swung out behind her.

"What do you mean?" I pushed myself back up straight and crossed my arms.

"I mean, you were in love with him, weren't you?" she asked. "Would you have listened if anyone told you he was full of shit?" She gave me a look like she expected an honest answer.

I wanted to give her one.

It took me a couple of moments to respond with,

"Probably not. I was head over heels for him. Ass over tits. I had doubts, I'd be lying if I said I didn't, but I ignored myself. Looking back, it seems so obvious."

I blew out a breath, frustrated with past me. "I talked about us moving in together but he always changed the subject. He was more interested in talking about singing a duet, or making an album together."

"Career stuff?" she said.

"Exactly," I agreed. "He never wanted to discuss us or a future together. When he talked about eloping, I thought it was spontaneous and romantic, and that somehow he got past his fear of commitment or some shit. I even suggested the timing was tricky because he had an album dropping a couple of weeks later."

I shook my head and laughed bitterly. "Even saying this out loud, I feel so stupid."

"Hey." She slipped off the desk and moved to sit next to me. "Not stupid, just naïve and in love."

"I guess so." I shrugged. "The sex was pretty awful anyway. He was all about his own satisfaction." At least he didn't take his time with it. The guys were a huge leap from that. A different planet.

"Now why does that not surprise me?" Violet said

dryly. "He sounds like a grade A prick to me. I wouldn't wish what happened to him on anyone, but I don't feel too sorry for him either."

"Neither do I," I admitted. "I would have been happy if someone slashed his tires or threw a rock through one of his windows. That would have been enough. But I'm not going to mourn his death. I'm not going to celebrate it either," I added quickly.

"Of course not," she said. "It takes a special kind of asshole to find pleasure in stuff like that. Someone like Zeke's brothers."

"How do you know about them?" I asked carefully. I had no idea how much she knew. I had to assume it wasn't much until she told me otherwise.

"My brother told me," she explained. When I looked questioningly at her, she added, "He's my stepbrother really. Levi Jones. His father is married to my mother."

She gave me a guarded look and I could tell exactly what she was thinking.

"That's cool," I said lightly. "I know you got signed to the label for your talent and not because you're related."

She relaxed visibly. "See, I knew you were awesome." She gave me a quick hug.

"Hell yeah I am," I said, mostly joking. I have

heard her sing, she is incredible. If anyone suggested Levi signed her because they were related, they could answer to me, and my guys.

15

TULLY

"I'M NOT ASKING you to do anything, just meet with me." My father's tone was insistent. When was it not?

I sighed and resisted the urge to throw my phone through the nearest window.

Xavier Lang was nothing if not persistent. He'd flown all the way from the other side of the country to see me, whether I liked it or not.

"Dad." I didn't remember when I started calling my adopted parents Mum and Dad, it just happened at some point along the way. I never took their last name, they hadn't asked me to, but they were my parents in every way that counted.

Including my privilege to rebel against them.

"We're flying out to Singapore in the morning," I said. Dad tried to pin me down for the last couple of days, including calling me when we were looking for Abbie.

I suspected that wasn't a coincidence. Dad was tight with Reuben. If Zeke's brother told him he sent Hunter and Parker after Abbie, Dad might have seen it as an opportunity to get my attention while I was distracted.

He of all people should know I wasn't easily distracted.

"Then you're free tonight," he said. "I know you don't have a concert."

That was information anyone could get with a quick Internet search. Evidently he assumed it meant I didn't have plans.

Okay, I didn't, not really, but I wanted to enjoy our last night in Australia before we left for Asia.

Not to mention, it was a rare night off. Could I get Abbie and I into Desdemona's again at this short notice?

"Maybe you can tell me what this is about," I said reasonably. "Over the phone." That didn't seem like too much to ask. He was busy, I was busy. We could chat quickly and get back to all the things.

"If I could do that, I would have called you from Sydney," he pointed out. "What I need to talk to you about, I need to do in person."

Fortunately for him, he couldn't see me give him an epic eye roll. Whatever he wanted could probably be done by email, but he wouldn't get his point across as well as he would while looking me in the eyes. That meant it was something important to him. As opposed to important to me. Our agendas were rarely the same these days. Were they ever? I guessed they were when I was young enough to still seek his approval. Those days were long gone, but not forgotten.

"If this is anything to do with me quitting the band and coming back to—" I started.

"Tully, you've made your feelings about that clear," he said evenly.

And yet, here he was, wanting to see me in person. It didn't take a genius to figure out he was up to something. Like most people, he always had an angle.

"You're not going to take me out are you?" I'd love to suggest I was joking, but if Reuben asked him to do it and paid him well enough, he'd at least consider it. In some ways, he was as bad as the evil twins, but Reuben's motives would have to match his. He was a minion, not a lackey.

He chuckled. "Only out to dinner. My treat."

Okay, if I didn't suspect something was up

before, I certainly did now. He never offered to pay for our meals. Or to be more specific, he was always happy to let me pay. I didn't mind, I had more money than I knew what to do with, but for him to offer sent up a shit ton of red flags.

"I can meet you for drinks," I said finally. "Before dinner. I already have plans for dinner and after dinner."

I'd have to think quickly if he asked me what they were, because I was lying through my teeth. Don't get me wrong, I loved the man and was grateful for all he did for me, but like Zeke, that life was behind me. If that meant turning my back on my adoptive family, then so be it.

"If that's all my son can give me, then that's what I'll take," he said, sounding testy. "It shouldn't take too long anyway."

It probably shouldn't, but that didn't mean he wouldn't drag it out as long as he could. He was never shy in reminding me he took me in when I was a kid.

I was surprised we got through a five-minute phone call without him mentioning it.

"Okay great." I gave him the name of a bar a few streets away. We could have had drinks in the hotel bar, but for some reason I didn't want him knowing where we were staying. That was silly, I knew. If Reuben knew where to find us, my father would.

And we both knew it.

He confirmed that a moment later when he said, "Okay, that's only a short walk for us both."

I realised he had the advantage, because I had no idea where he was staying.

Why did everything between us feel like a chess game? Move a piece, manoeuvre it into position, anticipate your opponent's next move, wait to strike.

Half the time, I was waiting for him to say checkmate.

Whatever, as long as he didn't try to take my queen.

I wondered what he knew about Abbie. I wasn't going to tell him much of anything, not until I heard what he had to say, and knew it wasn't anything bad.

For all I knew, it could be something totally innocent. Maybe he came all this way to ask me to teach him to play the guitar.

Okay, I didn't believe that either.

"You want me to swing by your hotel and pick you up?" I asked casually. "I know Perth better than you do." And then I would know where he was staying.

Of course, he saw right through the suggestion.

"No, that's all right, I'll meet you at the bar. Don't be late."

"When am I ever late?" I asked.

"There's a first time for everything, Tully. We'll all be late some day." He laughed.

I didn't. In spite of his assurances, it still felt like a veiled threat.

"I'll see you at seven," I said.

"Make it six," he said. "I'm an old man, I don't want to be out too late past my bedtime."

"You're not an old man," I assured him. "You're barely out of the egg." He loved fishing for compliments. It was his favourite hobby.

"Hundred year old egg," he said with a laugh.

This kind of silly talk made it feel like we were father and son, at least more than the rest of the conversation had. We always got along pretty well, but on his terms.

As long as they didn't interfere with my music career, or my other relationships, then I'd accommodate him.

I had a feeling whatever he wanted to discuss in person would overstep by a long way.

"I thought I could smell something nasty," I joked.

He snorted. "Thanks, Tull, love you too."

I chuckled. "I know you do, I'm awesome."

"You're certainly my favourite adopted son," he said.

"I know I don't need to point this out, but I'm your only adopted son," I said.

"Huh, you're right. How about that? I'm sure you'd still be my favourite even if I had a dozen," he assured me.

"Sure," I dragged the word out slowly. "It's easy to say that when you don't."

"When did you get so cynical?" he asked.

When my mother was murdered and my father went off the rails, I thought.

Out loud, I said, "I was born cynical. I think it's in my DNA or something."

"Something like that," he agreed. "I'll see you in a few hours."

"Yeah, see you in a bit." I ended the call and put down my phone as Zeke stepped into the room, dripping with sweat. I looked past him, but he was alone.

"Abbie is with the others," he said.

I nodded slowly. "Good." I already couldn't remember a time when I wasn't looking out for and worrying about her. The moment I met her I was fully invested in everything about her. She was easily the most incredible, beautiful and sweet person I ever met.

I was happy to wait as long as it took for her to be ready to be invested in me as well. That wait was one thousand percent worth it. The memory of smacking her ass with a paddle until it was red, then fucking her until we both screamed, was seared into my memory like a brand. The way she'd taken to the blindfold, and let me touch and feed her, was arousing as hell. Nothing, no one, ever came close.

Honestly, there was nothing about her that wasn't arousing and compelling. The way she looked, the way she spoke, sang, smiled and laughed; I felt like I'd known her for a thousand lifetimes the moment she walked into the studio on that first day. I had no doubt, not even a drop, that we would be together.

Fate said so, and who was I to argue with fate?

Yeah, I was falling for her hard.

"You okay?" Zeke crouched beside his suitcase and opened it. He pulled out some fresh clothes and put them aside. He must have just come from the hotel gym, or a run around the city.

I should have done either of those myself, but a song idea sprang to mind and I was busy scribbling down chords and lyrics until my father called.

"My father is in town." I told him about the phone call and my suspicion that he was up to something.

He slammed his hand against the floor. "That's it. We're buying an island and dropping out of civilisation. I'm done with these motherfuckers." He sighed through his nose and stood. "If only it was that easy."

"Yeah. Wherever we go, they would find us." Unless it was somewhere really, really remote, and I doubted we would give up streaming movies just to keep our families from hassling us.

Priorities.

Zeke pulled off his sweat-drenched shirt and tossed it aside.

I wasn't into guys, but I couldn't forget seeing him and Asher together. I wasn't blind, they were both good-looking guys, and watching them kiss and fuck was as hot as hell.

Me touching Abbie, Abbie touching me…

I could get used to sessions like that. Even Penn, who had only gotten himself off, wasn't complaining about it.

It was a new experience for us, but one I was certain we would do again.

And again.

And again.

Everything about it felt normal and natural, and

amazing. Although, there had to be a better environment for an orgy than a small hotel room.

I filed that in the back of my mind under things to think about when the tour was over.

"Are you going to meet with him?" Zeke asked.

"If I don't, he'll come here," I said. "I'm not ready for him to meet Abbie yet."

"If my family hasn't scared her off, your family won't," Zeke pointed out. He looked like he was barely holding back a smile.

"That's true," I agreed. "I'm almost certain my father won't kidnap her."

"Almost certain isn't certain," Zeke pointed out.

"That's what I'm worried about," I said. "Something about all of this is off."

"And by off you mean— What?" Zeke asked. He looked like he'd caught my unease.

"I don't know," I admitted. "It might be good, old fashioned paranoia." After a moment, I added, "And then, maybe it's not." My father obviously had some ulterior motive. The question was, was it innocent, or guilty as fuck?

Zeke looked frustrated but he nodded. "We'll be on high alert either way. They can reach us anywhere in the world, but the moment we leave Australia, it'll be that much more difficult for them.

They'll have international authorities to contend with."

We both knew there were ways around authorities anywhere on the planet, but potentially, coming after us would take them longer and cost them more money.

No, if they were going to do anything, it was more likely to happen here in Perth than anywhere else in the world.

Whatever they had in mind, they only had hours to do it.

"I should send Asher with you," Zeke said. He didn't look as though he liked that idea any more than I did.

I considered it for about half a second, then shook my head. "I can handle myself. If I turn up with Asher, Dad will know we're onto him. Besides, you might need him here."

"Yeah," Zeke agreed. "But I have an idea."

16

TULLY

I WAS RIGHT ON TIME, but my father was already waiting for me. He had that look on his face like he was *slightly* annoyed because I was *slightly* late.

Since I wasn't, I ignored his expression and smiled.

"Hey." I stepped over and gave him a quick bro hug.

He glanced down at my outfit and made no effort to hide his disapproval. "You're looking...well."

What did he expect? A three-piece suit? That wasn't gonna happen.

Instead, I wore my usual rock star uniform: jeans with holes in the knees, a faded Wolf Venom T-shirt, leather jacket and leather boots.

Personally, I thought I looked pretty fucking good.

Wasn't it a father's job to disapprove of what his son wore while in his mid-twenties anyway? I made a mental note to get myself a dinosaur costume to wear next time. He'd enjoy disapproving of that.

"Sorry, if I knew you were in town I would have gone out and bought a ball gown," I joked.

"Four hours' notice should be plenty to find the perfect dress." He smiled and waved towards a table in the back. "Maybe something bright yellow."

"Nah, yellow's not my colour." I slipped into the stool opposite him. "Maybe bright pink or dark red."

Yeah, right. If I was going to wear a ball gown it would be black. Since I would look absolutely ridiculous in it, I might as well be slick at the same time.

"Would you like something to drink?" he asked.

"I'll get it," I said. It wasn't that I didn't trust him to slip something into my drink…

Okay, maybe that was it, to some extent, but I didn't mind buying the old guy a beer or two.

He looked at me like he thought I was going to slip something into *his* drink, but he nodded. "You know what I like."

"Fast cars, good food and a successful business deal," I said with a grin.

An obedient son might not go astray either.

I slipped off my stool and headed to the bar. After a brief chat with the young woman behind the bar, who obviously recognised me, I grabbed us both a beer and sat his in front of him.

"I think she likes you," he nodded his thanks, then jerked his head toward the bar. "She hadn't stopped looking this way."

"Are you playing matchmaker now?" I sat back down and took a sip. "So, you want to talk to me about something? Other than my love life."

I didn't see any point in dragging this out any longer than necessary. If we could clear the air between us, maybe we could have a civil conversation like father and son.

"I have a business proposal for you," he said. Apparently he caught the same 'let's get this over with' vibe.

"Yeah?" I said casually. I was sure I wasn't interested, but I'd do him the courtesy of hearing him out before I told him to fuck off. "I'm all ears."

Usually that would have provoked a joking reply from him, such as only being able to see two ears.

This time, he just smiled faintly and sipped his own beer.

"I know you're not going to go back to the work you were trained to do," he said carefully. He was clearly mindful we sat in a public place.

Of course, people would notice if he stood up in his stool and shouted, "Hey, my adopted son is a trained assassin. How about that? Anyone need someone killed for them?"

There was a time and place for that and this was not it.

"Nope," I said simply and firmly. "I appreciate the skills my training gave me, but I'm not that person." I couldn't kill people for money. I didn't want to kill people for any reason.

"I understand." He wasn't happy about it, but that was his problem and he knew it. "I have something else in mind."

That had me immediately on guard. He never mentioned an alternative before. I couldn't guess what he had in mind.

"Yes?" I said carefully. "I'm listening. I can't make any guarantees about how I'll respond, but I'm listening."

The sides of his mouth drew back in displeasure,

but he nodded. "You may have noticed I'm not getting any younger. I might not be a hundred year old egg, but I'm starting to feel like one." He almost smiled.

"You're not that old." For the first time, I worried about the direction this conversation was going. Was he saying his time was limited or something like that? I was wary of his intentions at times, but I still loved the man. I didn't want to lose him.

"No, but I want to slow down at some point," he said. "And I want to hand my business dealings over to someone I can trust."

I blinked. Okay, I hadn't seen that coming.

"Wait, you want to hand your business over to me someday?" That had my head spinning. Parts of the Lang Corporation were actually legal. If I could strip off the stuff that wasn't, I might actually have a viable enterprise on my hands.

"Who else?" he asked easily. "As far as I'm concerned, you're my son. You're smart, competent and compassionate." He said the last word like it left a bad taste in his mouth. "Why would I not want you to work with me?"

"I can think of a few reasons," I said. "For one thing, if you sell off everything, you'll have a shitload of money to retire on. I thought that was your plan?"

"It was, until I realised I spent my lifetime

building something and don't want to sell it off to any old person." He took a gulp of beer.

"Sell it off to any young person then," I said, half joking. I didn't need his money. I didn't need to work another day for the rest of my life if I didn't want to.

On the other hand, running his business might give me something to do other than sit around and practice guitar, or sip cocktails on the beach.

Although, he could have a comfortable retirement and spend his own time drinking cocktails on the beach. Surely that was more fun than handing everything over to me?

"I don't want to sell it off to anyone." He rested his elbows on the table. "I want it to keep running. I'd like to see you run it and then hand it down to your children someday."

My children? Now there was an interesting concept if I ever heard one. I wasn't sure how I'd even begin to explain that to him.

Abbie might not want children, and with five other guys in the equation, I might never have one that was biologically mine. Of course, any child she had I'd think of as mine. If there was anything my adopted parents taught me, it was that biology isn't everything. A person can be a parent even if they aren't related by blood. Any child shared between the seven of us would certainly have an interesting life.

They'd never be short on love or money.

Idly, I wondered how long it would take them to learn that if their mother or one of their fathers said no to something, they could keep asking father after father until someone said yes.

Or they would go straight to Asher. If anyone said yes to them doing something they shouldn't, it would be him.

"So, what do you think?" Dad asked. "I haven't heard a 'no fucking way' yet."

I snorted softly and smiled. For some reason, hearing him swear was funny. Maybe because he was so straight laced and uptight most of the time.

"I haven't ruled it in or out," I said finally. "There's a lot to consider. I'm not done with the band yet. I don't know when I will be. I know you'd want me to learn the ropes before you hand over the reins to me. That could take a year or two."

He seemed pleased I was actually considering it. "We have time. I don't plan to step away for another ten or twenty years."

I nodded and sipped my beer in silent contemplation for a minute or two.

"What's the rush then?" I asked him. "Why fly all the way out here for this? You could have asked me at Christmas or at Mum's birthday." I always tried to get home for those, his birthday as well. I had to play the dutiful son once in a while.

He glanced at his watch.

A tingle passed up and down my spine. There was definitely something going on here. But what was it?

He looked back up. "I want to hand part of the business over to you as soon as possible. If only in name for now. The legal stuff takes time and I didn't want to wait to get started on it."

"What part of the business?" I asked carefully. I wasn't interested in the part that involved training and hiring assassins, and making sure they got paid. Or the money laundering.

"Believe it or not, I bought a record label not long ago. I thought you might be interested in having a say in how it's run." He swallowed another gulp of beer.

I stared at him. He'd surprised me so much, a small shove might have knocked me off the stool.

"You bought a record label?" If I was all ears for anything, it would be this.

"Which one?" I asked eagerly. I didn't try to hide

the fact my interest was piqued. I hadn't thought about running a label, but now he mentioned it, it might be exciting. I'd learnt a lot from Levi about how to do it right.

"Onyx Riot Records," he said.

My jaw dropped open slightly. Abbie's old label. That couldn't possibly be a coincidence. Not in a million years.

"I didn't know it was sold," I said carefully. I didn't keep up with that part of the industry, but if only for Abbie's involvement, I was surprised I didn't know. Did she?

Dad shrugged. "Apparently they've had some shady business dealings and the police and tax office were looking into them. A lot of their acts left when their contracts ended and they were going under. I picked it up for a song, so to speak."

I chuckled. "Good one."

"I thought so," he said smugly. "So, are you interested? You can pick executives to run it until you're ready to take over, but essentially it would be your baby. I'd be a silent partner, but I'm sure you could make me a lot of money."

"I'm sure I could," I agreed. "Can I have some time to think about it?"

"Of course, but why do you need time? I thought

this would be exactly your thing?" He cocked his head at me and looked irritated, like he was holding the hoop and expecting me to jump straight through.

"It is," I agreed. "Like you said, though, a lot of the acts left. The label's reputation isn't stellar right now." That was what Pietro Rossi got for screwing Abbie over. It seemed she wasn't the only one the label pissed off. "It would be a lot of hard work to build it back up to something reputable and profitable."

"If anyone can do it, it's you," he said. "Give it ten years and it will be the biggest, best label on the planet. Bands will be lining up down the street to sign with you."

"To be fair, bands line up down the street to sign with *anyone*," I said dryly.

Could I resist the opportunity to search out new talent and give them the same chances we had? Who wouldn't want to give back like that?

"They would do it even more for you." He glanced at his watch again, then sat back on his stool.

I had the distinct feeling whatever he brought me here for, he kept me just long enough.

Was it just long enough for Zeke to do what he planned?

17

ABBIE

"EVERYONE, get all your things together. We're getting the fuck out of here," Zeke said. His tone was calm, but with a heavy undercurrent of urgency.

"What the hell?" Penn stood with his shirt in his hand. Naked from the waist up, he was a wall of muscle like the rest of the guys. Muscle and tattoos, and hair damp from the shower. "We're supposed to be going out to dinner."

"Yeah, well, change of plans." Zeke grabbed his suitcase and nodded to me to get mine.

"What's happening?" Channing asked. He didn't look scared, none of them did, but Zeke's urgency was contagious.

Asher and Landon were already stuffing T-shirts into their suitcases and closing them.

"Maybe nothing," Zeke said. "Maybe something. In the event that it is in fact something, we're getting out of here."

"Tully just left," I pointed out. Something about talking to his adopted father. Whatever it was, he hadn't seemed happy about it.

"Exactly," Zeke said. "He suspects something is going to go down, so we're not gonna be here if that happens."

I opened the door to the adjoining room where my suitcase was. "Why would they make sure Tully wasn't here?"

Zeke followed me and started to shove Tully's things into his case. "Tully has a specific skill set. They won't want him here if they come after us. Don't worry," he flashed me a smile, "the rest of us have skills of our own. We'll be fine."

"But having Tully here would help us?" I asked. What the hell did he think might happen that we'd need an assassin for?

"It would help," he agreed. He hesitated and looked up at me. "I know Tull seems all sweet and zen and shit on the outside, but trust me when I say you don't want him pissed off at you. Mostly because you would never see him coming." He went back to packing up Tully's things.

"I don't know if I should be scared or find that hot," I said reflectively. "Maybe both."

Zeke chuckled. "Whatever you do, don't panic. They think we don't know what they're planning and that they'll catch us by surprise, but they won't. If I was really worried, I'd ditch our suitcases and shit, and run. I don't think that's necessary. We just need to relocate for the night, or fly out to Singapore if we can get a flight tonight. They'll turn up here to find us gone."

He sounded so certain, it went a long way to calming my nerves. The deep, lingering kiss he gave me once he finished packing Tully's stuff helped too.

"Trust me," he said softly, his fingers tangled in my hair.

"I do," I told him. "I love you."

"I love you too. Now let's get the hell out of here." He gave me a last kiss and reluctantly slipped his hands from me.

He grabbed the handle to my suitcase in one hand and Tully's in the other and hauled them through the door into the other room.

"Everyone stay here. I'm going to tell Blazing Violet to get out too. If something happens we don't want them to be collateral damage."

"Got it, babe," Asher told him. "Be careful."

"Always." Zeke kissed him, then ducked out the door and closed behind him.

Asher gestured for us all to move our suitcases to one side of the door, where we could grab them quickly.

"This is bullshit," Penn said. He pulled on his shirt, but his usual scowl was in place. "Can't we enjoy one night of peace without everything going to shit?"

"Apparently not," Landon said. "At least life isn't boring." He hooked an arm around Channing's waist and leaned against him.

"Yeah," Channing agreed. "If it was boring, you would complain about it."

"I fucking wouldn't—" Penn started.

"Maybe now isn't a good time to fight with each other," I suggested.

A sliver of fear crawled down my spine like a spider. If we were going to get out of this in one piece, we needed to be united and quiet.

"Abbie is right," Asher said. "Save the fighting for later, when we have some mud for you to roll around in."

The mental image of Penn rolling around naked in mud was almost enough to settle my fear. It was certainly enough to distract me for a couple of moments.

What were the chances that would happen in real life? Slim, I was guessing, but a girl could dream. Or at least fantasise.

The door knob rattled, making me jump.

"Let me in," Zeke's voice came from the other side.

Asher opened the door slightly and peered out. "How can we be sure it's really you?" he asked teasingly.

"Ha, fucking ha," Zeke said sarcastically. He shoved the door the rest of the way open and stepped inside.

Jackson was on his heels. "Are you sure they're coming for us?" He looked concerned but not scared.

I wondered what skills the band's manager had. For all I knew, he was a sniper or an accomplished getaway driver. Or had a black belt in some martial art. Or was really good at baking cakes.

What? When I'm anxious, I think about food.

"I'm not sure of anything," Zeke said. "Tully said his father was cagey as fuck on the phone, and this is a long way to come to be cagey. I'd rather be safe than sorry. The sooner we get out of the country, the better."

Jackson nodded, but didn't question Zeke's reasoning. "I found us a little hole in the wall place we can stay for the night. The kind where no one asks questions."

"Sounds like my kind of place," Asher said with a grin.

"Since when did you stay anywhere less than five stars?" Penn asked him.

"Plenty of times," Asher said. "Remember some of those fleabag places we stayed when we were first starting out?"

"I try not to," Penn said. "Some of those places were shitholes. I don't know how it's legal to ask people to pay money to stay in dumps like that."

"Who says it's legal?" Asher asked.

"Asher has a point," Landon said. He looked at me and added, "We did some dubious things back then."

"Just back then?" I teased.

He grinned. "She knows us too well already."

"Right." Zeke fixed us with a serious look. "Let's go."

He opened the door as Violet and her guys trudged up the corridor dragging their suitcases behind them.

"Just in time," Asher said.

"Better than coming late," Blaise said. "What the fuck is going on?"

"I'll explain everything when we get out of here," Zeke said. "You four take the elevator down. Jackson, you, Penn, Channing and Landon, go across to the other side of the hotel and take the stairs down there. Asher, Abbie and I will take the stairs down here, on this side of the hotel."

Everyone nodded and headed off where they were told. No one, not even Penn, argued.

At the same time, no one was rushing. We looked like we were casually leaving the hotel, nothing more.

Except—if we were casually leaving, we would all take the elevator down together. Wouldn't we?

Hell, if anyone asked, we could always say we needed the exercise. The guys didn't get as buff as they were without working at it. That included taking extra steps whenever possible.

Okay, that usually meant taking the steps up and not down, but close enough. Hopefully no one would ask.

I glanced over my shoulder as we headed for the stairs.

Penn looked back at me. For once, he didn't glare at me like something he might scrape off the bottom of his shoe. He gave me a nod, then turned and disappeared around the bend with the other guys.

I didn't know quite what to make of that, but then Asher ushered me to the door that led to the stairs, and Zeke took my suitcase.

"It'll be quieter if we carry them," Zeke explained. "And since you apparently carry bricks in yours, I'll help you out." He flashed me a grin.

I huffed and pretended to sulk. "Not bricks. Just several pairs of heels and a bunch of makeup."

"No clothes?" Asher grinned. "I knew you were my kind of girl."

"Mine too," Zeke agreed. "I can't wait to see you walking around just in heels."

"Ha ha," I said sarcastically. "Unfortunately for you two, there are clothes in there. Fortunately, you might convince me to just wear heels, if you ask nicely."

"Shhh." Zeke stopped walking so suddenly I almost walked past him.

I caught myself at the last moment and turned to face him. He seemed to be listening carefully for something.

I listened too, but couldn't hear anything. I mouthed, "What is it?"

He shook his head. "I can't hear anything now," he

whispered. "Let's walk as quietly as we can. No more talking."

Asher and I both nodded.

I put a hand on the rail for support, and pulled off my shoes. I'd move silently without them clicking on the concrete steps as I went.

We made our way down to the next landing in almost absolute silence. It was so quiet I heard my heart racing.

My mind was doing the exact same thing.

Zeke said Reuben didn't want him dead, because he wanted him to return to the family. What did that mean for the rest of us? I realised I assumed up until now that Reuben was involved, but what if he wasn't? What if this had something to do with the killer?

Hell, it might be some ploy by the press to flush us out so they could humiliate us in some way.

Okay, that was far-fetched, but I wasn't ruling out anything just yet. Not until I knew exactly what, if anything, we were up against.

It was possible Tully's father just wanted a chat and we were doing nothing more than jumping at shadows.

Honestly, I'd prefer to jump at shadows than be caught out if there was some plot against us.

Noise came from outside the door of the next landing.

We paused for a moment, but it was nothing more than music and people talking. I'd hate to be in a room near whoever that was. They weren't even playing anything by Wolf Venom, Blazing Violet or me.

Sad.

Zeke nodded at us to keep going. If he was straining carrying the two heavy suitcases, he gave no sign of it. He probably lifted more weight at the gym on a daily basis. He wasn't even sweating yet.

If it was me, my arms probably would have fallen off by now.

We crept past the door and down the next set of stairs.

I glanced over the railing. We had three more floors to go before we were out of the hotel. I hoped the others were okay. With any luck, Penn wasn't being an asshole and giving anyone an excuse to push him down the stairs.

I'd feel better when we were all together.

We crept past the last three landings and made our way to the door which should lead right outside. It would be locked from the other side, but being a fire escape, we should be able to let ourselves out.

Should being the key word here.

We reached the bottom and Asher put a hand on the crossbar. The door opened with only a squeak of protest.

Thank fuck.

That relief was short-lived.

Two familiar, identical faces greeted us.

"Going somewhere?" Hunter Brantley asked.

18

ABBIE

PARKER GRINNED AT ME. "Long time no see."

"What the fuck do you want?" Zeke snapped. He looked like he was ready to grab them by their hair and smash their heads together.

I wasn't sure I would try to stop him.

"Hey Ash," Parker said. "I haven't seen you for ages. How have you been?"

Asher shrugged. "Fine, thanks. You?"

Parker shrugged back. "Not bad. Keeping busy, you know how it is."

"Yeah, I do," Asher agreed. "I'd kinda like to know what the fuck you're doing here too. I mean, if you don't mind me asking."

"Would you believe we're here to help?" Hunter asked.

Zeke barked a laugh right in his face. "Not for a second, no."

"Ouch." Hunter turned to Parker and said, "That's not very nice. Is it Parker?"

"It really isn't," Parker said. "But we're actually legit. We were on the way to the airport when Reuben told us to turn around."

"Reuben told you to help us?" Zeke said in disbelief. "Why?"

"Tully's adopted father, Xavier Lang, has been dealing with the Fiorellis. Reuben thinks he's going to make a move on you to prove his loyalty," Hunter said. "And before you ask, no, it has nothing to do with the Bells. Lila knows nothing about it."

"Sure she doesn't," Zeke said. He shrugged. "We can take care of ourselves. You guys can piss off."

Parker pressed a hand to his chest, over his heart. "You hit me right here, bro. Fortunately for you, I don't follow your orders. Reuben said to help you and that's what we're going to do. That starts with getting out of here."

"It should start with being less predictable," Hunter said. "We figured out exactly where you'd come out. And when. And exactly with who."

Parker stared at him. "We did, too, didn't we? Fuck yeah. Go us." They shared a high-five.

"You're my brothers," Zeke said dryly. "You should have some idea how I think. Just like I have some idea how you think."

"Lucky you," I said sarcastically. To the evil twins I said, "Are we really supposed to trust you?"

"We're very trustworthy," Hunter said. "We said we would help you and we will. We said we wouldn't rape you, so relax."

Zeke growled low in the back of his throat. "If you little pricks touch her, I will rip off all four of your heads, one after the other."

"That's not very nice," Parker remarked.

"It really isn't," Hunter agreed.

Zeke leaned towards them. "Then keep your motherfucking hands to yourselves. I won't warn you again."

"I'd like to point out I would help him rip off your heads if you touch her," Asher said, his tone much nicer than his words.

"So will I," I said darkly.

"So will we," Landon said as he and the other four guys stepped around the side of the building towards us.

Channing nodded in agreement.

Penn looked at the twins like he would prefer to

bash their heads together and save the time ripping off any body parts.

I had to admire his train of thought if that was what he was thinking. It would be a lot quicker and easier.

"Oh look, they're multiplying," Parker said, looking completely unruffled.

Only Hunter laughed at his remark. "We should get out of here. I can't guarantee we won't be outnumbered. I don't know about any of you, but I'd prefer not to have that happen."

"I prefer that too," Parker said. "This way." He waved towards the street.

"Are we supposed to trust them?" I asked Zeke. Who knew what was waiting for us if we followed them? Just because there was a ring of truth to what the twins said didn't mean it was all true. It made sense that Tully's father would draw him away, out of trouble if someone was going after Zeke and the rest of us. Apart from that, it might all be crap.

"No," Zeke said. "But we were headed that way anyway. If they want to tag along, they can. But they can tag along in front of us, where I can keep an eye on them."

"The brotherly love is touching," Hunter said ironically.

"You fuckers kidnapped Abbie twice and you think I should trust you? Fuck that." Zeke gave them a withering look and picked up the suitcases before nodding at the twins to walk ahead of us.

"Only because we were ordered to," Parker said as if that made everything all right.

"If you were ordered to suck your brother's cock, would you do it?" Penn asked.

Asher responded with a choking laugh. "Good question."

"Which brother?" Hunter asked.

Penn stopped for a moment to stare at him. "Does it even matter?" He started walking again, shaking his head to himself while he muttered something about sick fucks.

Hunter shrugged. "I guess not."

He didn't answer the question, which was probably just as well. I didn't think anyone wanted to know. If he would do that, then who knows what else he would do?

We stepped towards the street which seemed darker than usual. A couple of streetlights were out near the front of the hotel. Were they like that last night?

"Everyone play it cool," Zeke said. "We're just leaving the hotel to go somewhere else."

"I'm always cool," Asher said. He was probably as on edge as I was, but he didn't look it. Neither did Zeke. In fact, all of the guys except Penn looked calm. Penn looked as agitated as always.

I doubted he knew the meaning of the word relax.

"Yeah, Asher is almost as cool as me," Landon said. "And I'm almost as cool as Channing."

"Ah, that's sweet," Channing said. "But you're much cooler than I am."

"Can we have this conversation when we're not tiptoeing through the streets of Perth?" Jackson asked.

"Yeah, what Jackson said," Zeke muttered. "Only, we're not tiptoeing. We're just walking along, minding our own business. Maybe waiting for a car to take us to the airport or some shit. Okay?"

"Wouldn't that make talking about who is the coolest fit into this scenario?" Asher asked. "For the record, it's me."

"I've always thought so," Hunter said. "Drums are definitely the coolest of all the instruments."

Asher turned his face towards him. "You really think so? Wait, I still hate you for what you did to Abbie." After a moment he added, "But you're right, they are the coolest."

"That's such bullshit," Penn said. "What's cool about smashing sticks against drums?" He rolled his eyes, but his tone was more joking than I had ever heard from him before. Presumably the guys razzed each other out a lot about having the best instrument. That was an argument they could have until the end of time and never have a resolution. They would always think their instrument was the biggest and best. Like their cocks.

"Only everything," Asher said. In the same tone of voice, he added, "Zeke."

"I see them," he said.

Landon stepped up beside me. "Don't look," he said softly. "Keep your eyes ahead, otherwise they'll know they've been noticed."

"Who is it?" I whispered. Because nothing says 'subtle' like a loud whisper.

"Dunno," Landon said. "I'm not looking either." He had one hand on his suitcase and slipped the other into mine. He gave me a reassuring squeeze, then kept hold of my hand. It felt as natural as holding any of the other guys' hands.

"Shouldn't there be a car waiting?" Zeke asked Jackson. He sounded like the perfect, spoilt rock star.

"You should know by now that I'm good, but I

can't perform miracles," Jackson snapped. He was also perfectly in his role as the hassled manager. "Let me call them."

"You do that," Zeke told him. He stopped at the edge of the road and put the suitcases down.

"It's so hard to get good help these days," Asher said.

"Depends how much you pay them," Parker said. "If you pay people well enough, you'd be surprised the things they will do for you."

"Like kidnapping?" I gave him a dirty look.

"And sucking off your brother's cock," Penn said. The keyboardist looked disgusted.

"We never said we would do that," Hunter said.

"You didn't say you wouldn't," Asher said. "Getting closer."

"Yep," Zeke agreed. They were both looking roughly over my shoulder, behind me. That wasn't disconcerting at all.

"Can you dance?" Landon asked.

I gave him a funny look. "Dance? I mean, I have some moves onstage."

"No, I mean like waltz." He left his suitcase where it was and put his hand on my waist. While I was still as confused as hell, he twirled me around, then swept me off to the side.

"What—"

I barely got the word out when Zeke was scooping up one of the suitcases and hurling it right where I was standing a moment earlier.

I hadn't seen the man coming up behind me, but I saw him now, as the case struck him right in the stomach. He staggered back, holding his torso and grunting in pain.

That would be why Zeke wanted us to bring our suitcases. I thought they might slow us down. It hadn't occurred to me he might use them as a weapon. Why would it? This whole crazy life was new to me.

"Fuck yeah." Parker punched the air. "That was epic, bro."

Zeke didn't look so impressed. "Friend of yours?"

He and Asher stepped towards the man who looked to be in a lot of pain. Of course, Zeke had thrown *my* suitcase at him. All those heels were bound to do some damage.

Fuck yeah.

"No one I know," Hunter said.

"Me neither," Parker agreed.

Zeke and Asher grabbed the man by his upper arms and hauled him up so we could all see his face.

"Does he look familiar to anyone?" Zeke asked. He looked around at us all.

I shook my head. "I've never seen him before, that I remember." I was half expecting it to be the guy who threw the can at me, but it wasn't. It would make sense if he was paid to do that to piss me off or get to Zeke, but I suspected he was just some random asshole. This guy on the other hand...

"Who hired you?" Zeke asked insistently. He shook the guy so violently I was surprised I didn't hear his bones rattle. As it was, Asher barely hung on to his other arm.

"Fuck off," the man grunted. "I was just minding my own business."

"So this isn't a gun in your pocket?" Asher asked.

While Zeke held the man still, Asher dug into his pocket and pulled out a small handgun.

"What do you know, it *is* a gun." He smiled and put it to the man's temple. "It's been so long since I've used a gun, my finger is getting twitchy." He could have been talking about the weather or the colour of his favourite T-shirt.

I should not have found what Asher was doing hot, but I did. He smiled, but the expression in his eyes was pure violence. I had no doubt he would kill the man to protect the rest of us. And the rest of us would help him bury the body.

"People will notice if you kill me out here," the man said.

Asher looked thoughtful. "That's true. That doesn't mean we can't kill you somewhere else." The sound of him cocking the gun echoed through the street. "On the other hand, I'm impatient."

"How about you don't kill him and he tells us how many people he's working with?" Zeke said. He sounded perfectly reasonable.

"I can work with that," Asher agreed. He poked the gun harder into the man's temple. "You know the question."

"Enough," the man growled. "You'll all be dealt with."

"Wrong answer, motherfucker," Asher said. "Try again."

"Fuck off." The man closed his eyes and braced himself.

Asher shrugged. "Thanks for bringing a gun with a silencer."

He pulled the trigger.

19

TULLY

"WHAT DID you really bring me here for?" I asked.

We'd spent enough time on pleasantries. Now Xavier needed to tell me the truth.

"A man can't give his son a record label?" Dad asked. He toyed with his empty beer glass as though he intended to use it as a weapon. We both knew he'd have to be faster than me if he did.

"It's a done deal, by the way," he added. "I've already had Onyx Riot Records transferred into your name. You're welcome."

"Why?" I kept a loose grip on my glass to match my posture. Most people would be fooled, but I knew he wouldn't. He knew I was ready to act in the blink of an eye if I had to.

Hopefully him knowing that would make it

unnecessary. I was younger, stronger and faster than him. And I had a feeling I had a fuck ton more at stake.

"Cut the crap. We both know you brought me here as a distraction."

He looked unruffled at the accusation. "And yet you came. Why would you do that if you were concerned about my motives?"

"Because if you're up to something and it involves my band, I know they can take care of themselves," I said easily. "What I don't know is why you'd be up to anything. You've been supportive up until now."

More than Zeke's family. More than a lot of families who preferred their children to chase solid careers, not dreams. Music was a tough industry. Most people didn't make it. It made sense for parents to want their kids to have a stable life and always know where their next meal is coming from.

"I am supportive of you," he said. "That's why you're here. But I have other interests as well, and those interests sometimes clash with yours."

"Meaning?" I wished he would just get to the point.

He took both hands off his glass and leaned forward to place his elbows on the table. "Meaning I'm doing business with a new partner here in WA.

Very lucrative business. So lucrative, one record label was a virtual drop in the ocean."

"Congratulations," I said carefully. There was a chance this new business venture was above board, so maybe this was a good thing and, like he said, he just wanted to give me something nice.

"Thank you," he said. "We'll all be a lot better off after this."

"After what?" I asked. "Can you stop talking in riddles and tell me what the fuck is going on?"

"The first rule of business is to get people to trust you," he said reasonably. "When you started out, you had to prove to your fans you could be consistent, right? And versatile. Otherwise, they don't know what they're getting and they won't bother with you. It's the same with any industry, creative or otherwise."

"Trust is an important commodity," I agreed. "In families as well as in business." That was my not subtle way of telling him he needed to be careful not to lose my trust.

"That's true," he agreed. "Sometimes you have to be ruthless to prove your trust to the other party."

"So you're here in Perth for a hostile takeover?" I asked. Those were an accepted part of business, even though they pissed people off at times.

He smiled slightly. "You could say that. My new business partner has a rival he'd like to put out of business."

That was nothing new either. Plenty of businesses wanted to push their rivals out of the marketplace. Destroy the competition and form a monopoly. It was a practice I wasn't interested in pursuing if I took over his business some day.

"What has that got to do with me?" I asked.

His long hesitation sent goosebumps all over my body.

"Dad?"

"His rival is Reuben Brantley. Dante Fiorelli doesn't only want to put him out of business, he wants to take them all out." He shrugged.

My blood went cold. The Fiorellis. I should have guessed it was something like that. They were bound to make a move at some point.

"All of them?" I echoed. Being right that something was going down gave me absolutely no satisfaction. What did was the knowledge Zeke would have gotten everyone out by now.

"You know Zeke wants nothing to do with his brother, right?"

"The apple never falls far from the tree," Xavier

said. "Either way, the decision wasn't mine. I'm doing what I have to do to look after our interests."

"*Your* interests," I corrected him. "I don't want anything to do with anyone who would want to kill Zeke Brantley." The rest of the family, maybe, but not Zeke.

"You're not seeing the bigger picture," Xavier said patiently, like I was an eight-year-old again. "He's collateral damage. We stand to become extremely wealthy from this business deal. I'm not asking you to stop doing your music thing, just don't stand in my way on this."

My hand tightened on my glass. "You want me to sit by and let you kill my friend? Because of money? Are you out of your fucking mind?"

"He's just one person," Xavier said. He looked like he was running out of patience now. "I'll deal with the rest of them over on the east coast. When that's done—"

I picked up the glass and slammed it down on the table so hard it shattered. "Will you listen to yourself? You think you can kill one of my best friends and my life is just gonna keep going on as normal?!"

"There is no reason why it can't," he said. "The band is still—"

"Not the band without its lead singer," I snarled.

"Not the same without our friend as a part of it. More than a friend, he's a brother to me. All of them are more family to me then you have ever been."

I was vaguely aware of shards of glass in my fingers, and blood starting to drip onto the table. Shallow grazes. Nothing that would stop me from playing, but I made my point.

His eyes flashed with anger. "After all I did for you, this is how you repay me? I've let you live your life and play around at being a guitarist, even after all the training your mother and I put you through."

"Training I didn't ask for," I hissed. "Training I was never suited to."

He responded to that with a chilling laugh. "You're perfectly suited to it. You just don't want to admit it. It's in your DNA. In your blood. Someday you'll admit that to yourself. When you do—"

"I will never admit that, because it's not true," I said, colder.

I could have been sitting across the table from a complete stranger. One who apparently had a hard time separating murder from money. One who seemed to have put his conscience aside. If he ever had one.

He sat perfectly still and looked at me across the table top. "Isn't it? Wouldn't you kill me right now if you had the chance? If you thought it would save your friend?" He lifted his chin in challenge.

I thought about it, and on some level, he was right.

But he was also wrong.

"In defence of my family, I would do anything," I said. "But I'm not going to kill you in cold blood. I'm not like you. Just like Zeke isn't like his family. Just like Asher isn't like his. Just like— okay, Penn is as uptight as his family. But the rest of us are our own people. I know you tried to mould me in your own image or whatever shit it is they say, but I'm not you or my father or my mother."

I referred to my biological parents now. How would I have turned out if they were still around? I might well have become the man Xavier accused me of being, but I hoped not.

I wanted to be so much better than my dark past, or my family's dark past.

"I will tell you this." I pulled out a couple of pieces of glass from my fingers and pressed my thumb against a deeper gash. "If you come after me or anyone else in the band, or anyone related to or close to the band, I will act in defence against you. And anyone you send after us."

"It's too late for that," he said. "By now, Zeke is

dead. My people had orders not to let anyone stand in their way. *Anyone.*"

Chills went through me again. "Meaning if I hadn't come here tonight…" Who the absolute fuck was this man? I had no idea who he was. Maybe I never had.

"I knew you would," he said. "There was never any risk."

"There was a risk," I said. "I had plans. I could have said no. Then who would you have left your business interests to? You would have made all that extra money, and for what?"

"Like you said before, I could have a comfortable retirement," he said easily. "I would prefer to hand things over to you but whatever happens, happens."

"Who wouldn't want a business built on the blood of his best friend?" I asked sarcastically. "You can shove it up your ass. And your fucking record label. I don't want your bribe."

"That's still a done deal," he said evenly. "Either way this goes down, it's in your name. It's yours to do whatever you want with. Or sell it. I don't care."

I wanted to tell him to screw himself and the label, but I knew the label would have employees and, if he dumped this on me, I would have to do something sooner or later.

When I calmed down, which might take quite a while after this conversation.

I could so easily pick up one of the bigger pieces of glass and cut his throat with it. Right here, right now. I might not feel bad about doing it.

Okay, he might be slightly right about who I really was. The difference was, though, I wouldn't act on my feelings of suppressed violence. Not unless I had to. That depended on him.

"This is where I tell you I never want to see you again," I said coldly.

I doubted he'd shed a tear if I was dead now, at the hands of whoever he sent after Zeke. I wouldn't shed a tear for him if he stepped out the door and was hit by a car. I might cry for the driver.

Fuck, I actually thought I loved the man. Right now all I had for him was disgust and anger.

"You'll change your mind when you realise how much I've done for you," he said. "How rich our family will be."

"There's more to life than money." It was easy for me to say, I had lots of it, but it didn't make me who I was. My music was more important to me than my bank account balance. Getting up on stage and making people happy meant everything to me. Doing it with people I loved was everything. The best, most important thing I could be doing with my existence.

"That's true," he said. "The one thing more important in life than money is power. The more money you have, the more power you can buy. With power, you can make real change. Think about that for a while." He rose from his stool. "Don't forget to call your mother for her birthday." Just like that his personality snapped back to the warm man he'd pretended to be all these years.

How did I not see through it sooner?

I didn't answer him. I turned and walked away.

My real family needed me.

20

"Fuck, I hate having brains on myself," Asher complained. He flicked at the front of his shirt for the hundredth time.

"Get changed then," Zeke said. "People are going to ask questions if they see you like that."

They talked so calmly, as if Asher hadn't blown a man's brains out a couple of minutes before.

Meanwhile, I was still trembling. Landon hadn't let go of my hand. Or I hadn't let go of his. I wasn't sure I could. The feel of his calloused skin in mine was the only thing keeping me from losing my shit right now.

Asher killed a man. Right in front of us. He hadn't even blinked. None of them had. No one but me. I was still trying to keep myself from vomiting.

Zeke caught the man and lowered him to the ground, while Asher wiped the gun with his shirt. When it was clean of his fingerprints, he shoved it into the man's pocket.

"We'll take care of this." Hunter and Parker lifted the man between themselves and carried him away like he was their drunk friend.

"You trust them to get rid of that?" Penn asked. He looked disgusted, as usual. It was impossible to tell what he thought about this whole thing.

Zeke shrugged. "Worst case scenario, someone sees them with a dead body. Not our problem. Our problem is keeping an eye out for more trouble. We need to find Violet and the others."

I almost forgot about the other band. Thank fuck they hadn't seen what I saw.

"Why do they call it a silencer?" I asked. There was nothing silent about it. Muffled, but still loud. The traffic roaring past the hotel must have covered the sound, because no one came running.

Unless they were hiding.

Fuck.

"They don't sound like they do in the movies do they?" Landon asked. "The movies get a shitload of things wrong. Especially that."

"Yeah." A man was dead and we were talking about movies? This was all sorts of wrong.

The worst part was, I didn't feel bad for the man Asher killed. He would have killed one of us and I doubt he would have lost any sleep over it. Witnessing it was horrifying, but I was already halfway to accepting it.

We stopped for a minute while Asher changed his shirt and shoved the dirty one into a rubbish bin.

With any luck, the bin would be emptied before they found the dead body. If they found it. If there was anything these guys and their families were good at, it was disposing of corpses.

I guessed it went with the territory.

"You okay?" Landon asked me. "You look rattled."

"I'm getting used to seeing death," I said. "But a killing that close up is a new thing for me. Are you not rattled?"

"I've seen all sorts of shit," he said. "That was relatively clean."

"Said the guy who didn't get brains on him." Asher pulled his clean shirt over his head and tugged down the hem.

"You were the one who grabbed the gun," Zeke said. "You can have a shower at the airport." Apparently he wasn't too worried about blood and brains, because he stepped over to give Asher a quick kiss on the mouth.

"Count on it." Asher kissed him back. "Maybe you and Abbie can join me." He deepened the kiss and ground his groin against Zeke's.

Trust him to be horny after killing a man.

"We should focus on getting the fuck out of here." Zeke reluctantly pulled away and adjusted his pants.

Asher sighed. "I hate cockblockers." He grabbed his suitcase and we headed to the front of the hotel where it was better lit.

"There you lot are." Violet stood with her guys outside of the hotel. "I thought you must have left without us."

"Nah, we got a little sidetracked," Asher said lightly.

"There's a taxi," Zeke said. "Violet, you and the guys take that and go to the airport. Jackson, go with them. See if you can organise an earlier flight, and make sure the rest of the crew are okay. We'll be right behind you."

I thought Jackson might argue, but after a moment he nodded.

"Abbie?" he asked.

"She stays with us," Zeke said firmly. "Don't

worry, we will get the next taxi. We'll be a couple of minutes behind you at the most."

Jackson's mouth was tight, but he gripped his suitcase and waved for the other band to head for the taxi in front of him. "Stay safe."

"You too," Zeke said.

We all kept watch while they climbed in. I don't think anyone breathed until the taxi pulled away into the traffic. I certainly didn't.

"Now would be a really good time for another taxi," Asher said.

"We could call for one?" I said. Figures there was never one around when you needed one the most. Unless you were at the airport. There was never a shortage of them there. That wasn't helpful, since we had to get there first.

Zeke pulled out his phone and tapped at the screen. "Looks like it's going to be at least ten minutes. Keep your eyes out for any trouble. That first guy was sloppy. Another one might not be."

We formed a loose circle, back-to-back to cover every possible angle.

I faced the road, to keep an eye out for the taxi. I knew what to look for with one of those. With an attacker, they could look like anyone. They didn't exactly walk around with a big sign on their forehead saying, 'I've come to get you.'

Of course not, that would be way too convenient. Jerks.

The longer we waited, the more sweat gathered on my palms and under my arms. Landon didn't complain about holding my sweaty hand, but it couldn't have been comfortable. I was glad he didn't let go. I was about ready to run into the traffic, pull over the first car and tap on the window to insist they take us out of here.

Since that shit didn't go down well in movies, then I assumed it wouldn't go down very well in real life either. With my luck, I'd probably get *run* down.

"Hey," Asher moved to stand beside me. "I'm sorry you had to see that. You know that shit doesn't happen very often, right? I usually don't go around killing people."

"I know," I said quickly. "It was him or us. I just—"

"Seeing someone shot in front of your eyes isn't nice?" he suggested.

"Not nice is an understatement." I looked at him intently, searching his face in the glow of the streetlights. I realised how little I knew him. How little I knew any of them. I mean, if I had to guess, I would have thought Zeke was the one most likely to kill someone. Seeing Asher do it sent my mind into a spin.

"I'll understand if you don't want anything to do with me," he said softly. "If seeing that side of me is too confronting."

"It's not like that at all," I said quickly. "What you did...it doesn't change how I feel. I need to get my head around it, that's all." After a moment, I was forced to admit, "It...it was kinda hot."

"But people coming after us isn't?" he guessed.

"It really isn't." I nodded. "I can't think of anything less hot."

"Not even Penny in his underwear?" Asher grinned.

"Me in my underwear is hot," Penn growled. "Almost as hot as me out of my underwear."

Now there was a mental image to make my panties wet. Fuck, with everything that was going on, these guys could still make me hot as hell. Wasn't there a law about that or something? If not, there should be.

Oh, right, the guys would break it anyway.

"That's true," Asher agreed. A fraction of a second later, he added, "Zeke, are you seeing what I'm seeing?"

"Yep," Zeke said. "Taxi is three minutes out." He

tucked his phone away and crossed his arms like he was impatient, but unaware of anything out of place around us.

"What are you looking at?" I managed to keep myself from glancing around wildly. So far, all I saw was traffic gliding past. It was starting to thin as it got later in the night.

"There's a few people, I count three," Asher said. "Right now, they look like tourists, but they look cagey as fuck to me. It's a matter of knowing what to watch out for."

"Right." Was that a skill I would learn with time? Hell, was it one I wanted to learn? I didn't want to think nights like this would become normal. At some point, I wanted a regular life, without looking over my shoulder for people with guns or drugs, ready to shoot me or threaten me or any of the guys.

"Dude with a cat T-shirt," Penn said.

"That makes four," Zeke said.

I spotted a car with a taxi sign on its roof as it slid around a corner. "I don't know if it's ours, but a taxi is coming."

"Get ready with your suitcases," Zeke said.

I wasn't sure if he meant to get ready to get into the taxi, or throw them, but he had the handles of his and mine in either hand. Every muscle in his body looked poised and ready.

"Girl with black jeans," Channing said. "She looks harmless, but I used to date a girl who looked like that so…"

"Always be suspicious of anyone who looks like your ex," Asher agreed.

"I would definitely be suspicious of anyone who looked like any of your exes," Penn said. "Mine too, come to think of it."

"We both had dubious taste in the past," Asher said. "Lucky that's in the past."

I made a note to ask about that later. Although, I doubted their exes were as horrible as mine. That was a pretty high fucking bar.

The taxi started to slow and came to a stop at the curb right in front of us.

"Thank fuck," I muttered. I went to open the door.

"Wait," Zeke said. He trotted around to the driver's side and leaned in to talk to the driver. After a tense minute or two of waiting, he straightened up and nodded. "Okay, get in."

"Quickly," Landon told me. He opened the door and pushed me inside, while Channing put their suitcases in the back of the car.

The guys hurried to do the same with the rest of the suitcases and Asher slid in on the other side of me. Penn sat by himself in the third row of the long SUV and Zeke climbed in beside the driver.

"What was that about?" I whispered to Asher. Could he tell if the driver was dubious by just talking to him?

"Zeke was watching to see what our would-be assailants would do," Asher whispered. "My guess is they melted back into the shadows when we started to get into the taxi. This is much too public of a place for them to attack us. The taxi has security cameras all over it and a radio to call for help faster than we could grab out a phone."

"Does that mean we're safe?" I asked.

"Not until after wheels up," Asher said reluctantly. "We can breathe a sigh of relief when we're in the air."

That wasn't what I wanted to hear, but at least he was honest. The question was, where was Tully?

21

TULLY

I DIDN'T bother to check the hotel room, they would have been long gone by the time I got there.

Instead, I dropped from a trot to a walk half a block from the hotel and moved silently through the shadows.

This, right here, was one of the reasons I preferred black. Also, it looked good on me.

Part of my training involved learning to keep myself from being seen. And if I was seen, to keep myself from being noticed. Okay it was difficult to avoid being noticed when people knew who I was just by looking at me, but before I was famous, I was good at blending in amongst the crowd.

Now, I had to be content with blending in amongst the shadows.

All of my instincts told me danger was right in front of me. Almost close enough to smell. To taste. To hear.

Unfortunately, night vision goggles weren't standard issue uniform for rock stars. I made a note to discuss that with Jackson and Zeke. We could start a new trend.

Okay, probably not. I should stop distracting myself with useless thoughts. I shouldn't have had that beer with Xavier. I should have stayed with the band and Abbie. They should be at the airport by now, at least on their way there.

A shuffle up ahead was faint, but unmistakable.

I stopped mid-step.

"This fucker is heavy," a voice said.

I frowned. I knew that voice. And if he was here—

"Maybe you need to lift more weights," said the other twin.

Yep, there he was. What the fuck were the Brantley twins doing still in Perth? And who were they carrying? My heart skipped a couple of beats. My mind raced ahead.

Was it Abbie or one of the guys? If it was, this was the evil twins last night breathing. They wouldn't hurt a hair on any other members of my family.

I started forward slowly, focusing on the sound of their voices and movement. They didn't seem to be trying to hide their presence. Or if they were, they weren't doing it very well. Both of them knew better than to be that sloppy. They must be feeling confident.

That was cause for concern.

I made out two shapes in the dark. No, three. One was lying on the ground at their feet. Who was that?

"I need to learn that move," one of the twins said.

I thought it was Parker.

"You already know how to shoot someone in the head," Hunter said.

Parker chuckled. "I meant the suitcase. The way Zeke threw the suitcase at this asshole was pretty fucking epic, don't you think?"

Hunter scoffed. "I could do that. Easy. Probably better than Zeke too."

"No offence, bro, but Zeke is taller and stronger than us. He could probably throw us better than you could throw a suitcase." Parker sounded admiring.

I frowned. What did all of this mean? Had the Brantley twins got wind of what my father and

Dante Fiorelli were cooking up and decided to team up? That made a twisted amount of sense. Reuben was an asshole, but he didn't want his brother dead. And Zeke didn't want to get dead. If he had to work with his brothers to achieve that, he might.

"I didn't know Asher had it in him to shoot someone in the head like that," Parker added. "His big brother would be proud of him."

That wouldn't be good news for Asher. Wait. Did he say Asher shot someone in the head? Was that who was lying on the ground? There were a couple of ways to find out, but one included waiting, and the other meant confronting the twins right now.

Since I wasn't afraid to take them both on by myself, I stepped out of the shadows as though I hadn't been standing there listening. In fact, I might have swaggered like I was out for a stroll.

"Evening," I said casually. I chuckled as one of the twins jumped in fright.

"Fucking hell," Parker said. "Where did you spring from?"

"Here and there," I said lightly. "What's happening?" Apart from them looking suspicious as shit. I took a half a second to glance down. I didn't know the man. Presumably the hole in his head was from Asher, if what the twins said was true.

"Apart from trying to save our brother from your father?" Hunter asked. "No, that's about it." Judging from the tone of his voice, he was wondering if I was in on it with my father.

"My father, as you call him," I said slowly, "has been telling me about how he's no longer aligned with your brother. Reuben that is." I knew they knew that, but I added it anyway.

Before they could jump to any conclusions, I added, "I told him my loyalty is with Zeke, not him. I don't give a fuck who he's in bed with, whether it's Reuben or Fiorelli. Frankly, anyone who comes after my friends is my enemy."

Even if that meant I had to work with shitheads like the twins.

"Anyone who comes after our brother is our enemy," Hunter said. "I guess that makes us friends." He crouched to pull something out of the dead man's pocket. In the dim light, I recognised a gun.

I snorted a laugh. "That's a stretch. Where is Zeke? And the others?" Was Abbie okay?

I held my hand up before they could answer. There it was again, the scuffle of footsteps.

"There were others with him?" I whispered.

"Without a doubt," Hunter whispered back.

"Then you should know, they weren't just after

Zeke. They'll kill any Brantley they find." After what they did to Abbie, I should probably slip away and leave them to their fate, but if Zeke worked with them, maybe they were redeemable.

Okay, that was the second big stretch of the last five minutes, but any trouble between them and whoever was coming would give me a chance to get further away.

"Well, that's not very nice," Parker said. "For the record, the others went to the airport. We decided to take care of this asshole to give them time to get out of the country."

"We need to get out of the state," Hunter said.

"We all need to get out of here," I agreed.

Before we could take a step, the light from a phone shone on us all.

I blinked against the sudden glare.

"Look, a two for one," said the voice behind the phone. A man around the same age as me, I guessed.

"Three," said another voice. "The boss said if his son gets in the way it's too bad."

"Tully." Hunter threw me the dead man's gun and pulled out one of his own.

I caught it and ducked out of the light. I raised the gun and aimed it at the man who held the phone. I squeezed the trigger.

"Shit!" The phone dropped to the ground and the light went out. The man clutched his arm.

There, that was better. It was hard to get a kill shot with the light in my eyes.

Without it—

I squeezed the trigger again and the man dropped.

"Shit, dude," Parker said. "That was epic."

"Yeah." I ducked down into the shadows. There were at least another two of them and no doubt they were armed. "We should go."

I listened, trying to discern exactly where the other assailants were. When the first shot rang out, I heard a shuffle of feet as they'd retreated. I wasn't sure exactly how far. No more than a metre or two. Three at the most.

"Going sounds like a plan," Hunter agreed. He ducked as a shot rang out. It hit the wall right where he had been standing. Good to see he was smart enough to know speaking would make him a target.

I reached out with my foot and kicked the phone in the direction I guessed the attackers went. Footsteps moved in response.

I hated guesswork, even educated guesswork, but I raised the gun and took the shot.

Judging by the grunt and a moment later, a thud,

my third bullet found its mark. How many did I have left? I couldn't be sure, but that last attacker would have a fair idea where I was right now.

I slipped out of the shadows and moved as swiftly and silently as I could to the other side of the alley.

A shot rang out, striking the wall where my head was a second ago.

Not today asshole, I thought.

I raised the gun to fire back, but one of the twins got a shot off first.

The attacker let out a howl of pain and rage. Not a kill shot then. Enough to distract the man.

"Let's go," I hissed.

I turned and moved towards the entrance of the alley, mindful there might be other attackers at this end too.

I paused a few metres from the entrance.

Someone was there. At least one. They weren't moving but I almost heard them breathing or thinking. Something.

Put it down to well-trained instincts if you want, but I knew.

I put out a hand to stop the twins and hoped they would see it and whoever was waiting didn't see me. I heard the smallest sound of surprise from one of them, but they stopped. I should have known Zeke's brothers would be as good at this shit as he was.

Alone, I started forward again. I kept every sense open wide. Especially the one that told me my life depended on me being careful. Xavier had written me off, but I wasn't done yet.

My finger lightly on the trigger, I kept the gun aimed forward, letting my instincts point it, and me in the right direction.

There were two people there, waiting. One just inside the alley, to the left. The other maybe two metres away, to their right.

I visualised the way they stood and waited, guns in their hands. I pictured their posture, the way they held their heads. They would be listening, the way I was. But they wouldn't have had my training. There was being quiet and careful, and then there were the skills of an assassin.

The two couldn't compare.

The question was, how many bullets were left in the gun? If any. If it was none and I tried using it, I was screwed. If it was one, I could take out one of the enemies, but then I'd have to contend with the other one. If it was two, piece of cake.

The problem was, I couldn't guess. Guessing got you killed.

I stopped and tucked the gun into my back pocket. Yeah, I know, don't put the gun in your pants, but I had nowhere else to put it.

I dropped down low and kept moving forward. My first target—the person on the right. The one on the left was already inside the alley. They would be easier to pin down once I took out the first one.

I circled slowly around until I was behind the person on the right. Another man, judging by their size and shape. They still faced the alley, waiting for us to appear.

You're out of luck, fucker, I thought.

I surged forward, hooked an arm around his neck and the other over his mouth. With the right amount of pressure, I was able to wrench his head to the side, twisting and breaking his spine. His death was almost silent. The only sound was the scuffle of his feet on the ground.

I lowered him down as the other would-be attacker turned.

His face was caught in the light of a distant window. I saw his mouth form an O of surprise and the fear in his eyes. The glint of the gun in his hand as he raised it towards me.

"Tully—"

I struck Xavier with an uppercut he taught me,

the heel of my palm smashing into the bottom of his jaw. His head snapped back so hard he only had time to make a terrified gurgle.

"Thanks for the training," I said as he started to fall.

I grabbed him but I had no remorse as I lowered the body of my adopted father to the ground.

22

ABBIE

"WE'RE on the flight out in ninety minutes," Zeke said as he slipped into the chair beside me. "We have thirty minutes to check in our bags and go through airport security into the lounge area." He rubbed a hand over his forehead and sighed heavily.

I felt as tired as he looked. "I can't wait to get out of here. Perth was one of my favourite places to visit, but now..." I couldn't get out of the city fast enough.

"Yeah." He tucked an arm around me and settled me so my temple rested against his chest. "At least no heads turned up without their bodies."

I let out a choking half laugh. "Just bodies with their heads." I glanced over to where Asher sat, talking in a low voice to Landon. I couldn't hear what they were saying, but they both looked as cheerful and light-hearted as ever.

Anyone watching them wouldn't suspect a thing.

Asher must have sensed me looking, because he turned toward me and grinned.

Did he really have to be so fucking hot?

Yes, yes he did. I still couldn't believe he cared about me as much as I cared about him. I was nothing special, just Abbie Hart, the singer who went through some rough times but managed to come out the other end more or less intact.

But here I was, sitting in Perth airport, having watched one of my boyfriends kill a man, after another threw a suitcase to disarm him. Tully was fuck knows where, and everyone else was acting like it was just another day in Wolf Venom.

A sensible person would run for the hills. All I could do right now was worry about the band's lead guitarist, and count my blessings I met the guys.

"At least we know who did it this time," Zeke said. "No mysterious stalker."

"Just a mysterious drummer." I smiled back at Asher.

Zeke's chest rumbled as he laughed. "You think Asher is mysterious?"

I looked up at him. "Not as mysterious as you."

The smile he gave me was both heart and panty melting. Fuck, these guys were going to be the absolute end of me.

"I'm not mysterious," he said. "I'm just a regular guy who is in love with you. And I kinda sing okay."

"I love you too," I said warmly. "You sing amazing but there's much more to you than that. Every day I find out new things about you. Just in the last couple of hours, I found out you throw suitcases. You didn't even break it."

"You're welcome." He leaned forward to kiss my nose. "Every day I learn new things about you too. I look forward to a lifetime of finding things out."

My heart fluttered at the idea of a lifetime with him. That sounded just about perfect.

"I want that too," I said softly. After a couple of minutes of silence, I broke it by saying, "How long do we have?"

He rolled his hips to the side so he could pull out his phone and check the screen. "Twenty minutes." He put his phone away and looked towards the entrance to the airport. "I don't want to leave without—"

"Tully," Channing said.

"Exactly," Zeke agreed.

"No." Channing stood up and waved. "Tully!"

I rose and looked in the direction he pointed.

Sure enough, Tully was weaving his way through the crowds.

He looked terrible. He was as hot as hell, as always, but his clothes were rumpled and his eyes looked haunted.

I trotted a few steps to close the gap between us, and threw my arms around him. He embraced me so tight I thought he might never let go.

"Are you all right?" The question was rhetorical. He was clearly not all right.

"Nope," he said softly in my ear. "But I will be. Thank you."

"What for?" I asked.

"Being you." He kissed me on the mouth, tasting my lips with his tongue, before he drew back and offered a faint smile.

He kept one arm over my shoulders and glanced past me. "You clowns better have brought my suitcase." He sounded like himself again, although the hardness in his eyes was unchanged.

All of the guys exchanged glances.

"Did anyone think to bring Tully's suitcase?" Asher asked. He scratched the side of his head. "I mean, I guess you can buy stuff in Singapore. Or in one of the shops in the lounge before you leave."

Tully sighed.

Asher grinned. "Just kidding. Of course we brought yours. We don't leave anyone behind and that includes dragging their shit along with us."

Tully shrugged. "I would have shared your stuff with you. We're about the same size aren't we?" He tilted his head as though sizing Asher up.

"Nah," Asher said lightly. "My underpants are way bigger. They have to be."

"Dream on," Penn said. He was the only one still sitting in his chair. He gave Tully a nod, then went back to scrolling through his phone.

"Jealousy is a curse, Penny," Asher told him.

Penn ignored him.

"Hey," Zeke greeted Tully. "It's good to see you in one piece." He gave the lead guitarist a bro hug. "What took you so long?" His tone was light but what he was asking was obvious.

"Tidying up some loose ends," Tully said. "Your brothers say hello by the way. We helped each other out a bit. They needed to clean up some more, and then they're headed back to Sydney. They're satisfied most of the loose ends are tied up for now."

He closed his eyes and let out a long breath through his nose. "Xavier Lang won't be a problem anymore."

"Fucking hell," Zeke said softly. "Are you sure?"

"I handled it myself," Tully said.

I frowned. "Is that…"

Tully nodded. "My adoptive father. It was him or me."

That explained the haunted look in his eyes.

"Oh, my god," I whispered. "Tully…" He killed his adoptive father? How was he keeping it together? I would be a complete mess.

He squeezed my shoulders. "He came after my family and didn't care if I was collateral damage. It is what it is. Now, don't we have a plane to catch?"

"Yes we do." Zeke clapped him on the shoulder. "We have ten minutes to check in. Let's get going. Everyone keep your eyes open. There might be another loose end or two out there."

We hurried to grab the handles of our suitcases and drag them towards the check-in counter. Fortunately, at this time of night, there wasn't much of a queue. We only had to wait behind a couple of other people before, one by one, we passed our suitcases through and had a tag with our destination woven through each of the handles.

With Tully on one side of me and Zeke on the other, I stepped through airport security without a ping. Presumably no one put a tracker on me.

Yet.

We walked through to the lounge and made our way down to gate sixteen. It was so quiet, we managed to get seats together, but away from everyone else.

While we waited to board, Tully told us about his conversation with Xavier and altercation with the assailants and the Brantley twins.

"How far behind us do you think they'll be?" Asher asked.

"Hunter and Parker?" Zeke asked. "I'd like to say they'll be on their way back to Sydney by morning, but honestly... Probably the flight behind ours."

"Is there any chance they'll keep protecting you?" I asked.

He shrugged. "If they're told to, they will. If they're told to fuck with us, then that's what they'll do. With any luck, Dante Fiorelli will keep them distracted for a while longer. I like it better when they're on our side."

"Yeah, I didn't want to have to kill them," Tully said. "There's been enough killing tonight."

"More than enough," Landon agreed. "Any more of it and Channing and I are going to start feeling left out."

"I don't think killing is something you need to join in on," I said dryly.

"I'd prefer not to," Landon said. He was leaving something unsaid, but I decided not to ask what it was. Another time maybe. The last few hours were overwhelming enough without learning some dark secret from the blue haired bassist too.

"Did it cross your mind I might be feeling left out too?" Penn asked. He frowned at Landon.

Landon scratched his chin. "Did you want to take part?"

"Not particularly, no," Penn said. He went back to looking at his phone.

Landon and Channing shared a look and shrugged.

"There you are," Jackson said as he and the other band appeared from another part of the lounge. They were carrying boxes of food and trays of paper coffee cups. "I figured you'd be hungry."

"I could eat," Asher said.

"Now you mention it, I'm starving," Channing said.

I wasn't particularly hungry after what I saw and what Tully told me, but I needed to eat. We all missed dinner and it was nearly eleven o'clock at night.

Jackson and Blaise handed out boxes of burgers and cups of coffee.

I would gratefully drink the coffee at least. Thank fuck it existed.

Once I opened the cardboard container with my burger inside, I realised I was hungry after all. The smell hit my nose and my stomach rumbled.

Asher raised his cup towards Jackson to toast him. "Best manager ever. Who else would remember to feed us?"

"Every manager," Jackson said dryly. "I wouldn't be good at my job if I let the label's star act starve to death.

"You wouldn't be very good at your job if *you* starved to death," Violet pointed out.

"That too," he said around a mouthful of burger. "Are we good?"

"For now," Zeke agreed. "I'll feel better when we're in the air. Until then, play it cool but keep your eyes open." He bit into his burger like he hadn't eaten for days.

To him, it probably felt like he hadn't. He was a big guy with a healthy appetite. He burned it all off onstage, so he could afford to eat whatever he wanted.

Maybe I should be more energetic. I could eat more donuts.

Jackson nodded, then turned to Tully. "All good with you?"

"Good enough," Tully agreed. "Better for having this." He nodded towards his dinner. "I might have a bottle or two of wine when we get to Singapore."

"I'm in," Asher said. "But make mine beer."

"We could all use a night out," Zeke said. "One that ends better than this night out did."

"What could be better than sitting in an airport eating hamburgers?" Landon asked. "Surrounded by my brothers, sister and Abbie. We made it this far."

"I'll drink to that." I toasted him with my coffee cup.

"I need something stronger than coffee," Penn grumbled.

"Don't we all," Tully said. "As long as it's not stronger than alcohol."

While Penn gave him a dark look, I gave Tully one of surprise. That was the first time anyone alluded to Penn's past since that article Zeke stopped me from reading out loud when we first met in the studio.

"No one is having anything stronger than alcohol," Jackson said firmly. "Eat up, we'll be boarding soon."

While I finished my burger, I watched Penn. He looked more pissed off than usual. And something else.

He looked troubled.

23

ABBIE

"I can't help noticing we haven't upgraded to private jets yet," Asher said as we were waiting in line to board the plane.

"Are you kidding?" I was feeling a lot better, having eaten. "Still no king-sized bed? How is that even legal?"

Considering everything I saw tonight, having a plane without a big bed was the most legal thing to have happened. That included those burgers. I wasn't sure anyone should be eating shit like that. It couldn't be good for us. Hell, I could say the same about coffee and alcohol, but life was too short to deprive yourself too much. Right?

"You're all shockingly deprived," Jackson said ironically.

"You said depraved wrong." Asher grinned.

"That too," Jackson agreed. "I'm not sure if it counts if you're proud of it."

"Of course it does," Asher said. "Admit it, that's one of the things you love the most about us."

"Yeah, it has nothing to do with how much money we make for him in the label," Landon said with no hint of resentment.

"Nothing at all," Asher agreed. "Our awesomeness might also play a part."

"It certainly isn't your modesty," Jackson told him. He showed the flight attendant his phone with his boarding pass on it, and was waved ahead of us.

Rather than following Violet and her band onto the plane, he stood and waited for us. He didn't bother to hide his concern. His eyes were glued on the space behind us, watching for trouble.

Every so often, I looked over my shoulder, waiting for someone to jump out at us. Or hand me a box containing a head. Or throw a can at me or even just an insult.

The flight staff did nothing more than glance at me and my boarding pass before they waved me forward. For the most part, their eyes were on the guys.

"Great show last night," one of them said. She was

a gorgeous brunette, with legs for days and perfect makeup.

There I was, dressed in a knee length skirt and a singlet top, my hair wound up into a messy bun. They probably assumed I was a tour staff, or one of the guys' sisters. Either way, I felt frumpy and plain next to this woman.

"Thanks." Asher grinned at her. "We had a lot of fun. Perth is always amazing. The label is forever saying, *come on, you guys don't want to play there, it's so far away from everything else*. But we always insist, right Zeke?"

"Fuck yeah," Zeke agreed. He also gave the woman a warm smile. "It's awesome over here. I wish we could spend more time."

"I wish you could too," she said in a flirtatious voice that made me want to punch her in the face. "I'd be happy to show you around next time you *come*."

"That would be great," Asher said. He elbowed Zeke. "You hear that, babe?"

For the first time, the flight attendant looked uncertain. She clearly hadn't expected that from two big, muscular guys with a reputation for being with a different woman every night.

"I did," Zeke said. He seemed to be enjoying

himself all of a sudden. He draped an arm over Asher's shoulder. And then, for good measure, he draped one over mine.

I was starting to feel sorry for the flight attendant, who didn't know where to look now.

"We should get on board," Zeke said. "Wouldn't want to delay the flight."

The attendant shook her head. "Um, Yes, right. We wouldn't want that." She looked at me like I was from another planet. Her eyes widened further when Tully stepped to the other side of me and took my hand.

I just smiled at her and shrugged. Somehow, the guys managed to make me feel beautiful, even when I was looking scruffy as shit. It was just another one of their many, many charms.

I managed to ignore the whispers of both flight attendants as we stepped away into the tunnel and headed into the plane.

"You guys are shit stirrers," Jackson said. "You know that, right?"

"What?" Zeke asked. "She was flirting with my boyfriend in front of my girlfriend. What was I supposed to do? Weren't you the one who said there's been enough violence tonight?"

"That was me," Landon said.

Zeke nodded slowly. "So it was. My bad."

"I had to step in, because Abbie is my girlfriend too," Tully said. He smiled at me with his beautiful, wide mouth and squeezed my hand.

That was the first time he called me that. I liked the way it sounded. It seemed now I officially had three hot boyfriends. Maybe it should have felt more complicated, but it didn't. It felt right, natural and incredible. I wouldn't change a thing about it.

"Of course you did," Penn said. "None of you can help yourselves."

"It's not my fault if I'm irresistible," I told him.

He snorted. "You said irritating wrong."

"How much longer are you going to be an insufferable asshole?" I asked him.

"How does until the end of time sound?" he retorted.

"About accurate," I replied. "Maybe you should try not being a dickhead once in a while. You might surprise yourself by enjoying it."

"I did try it once," he said. "Worst thirty seconds of my life."

"I'm surprised you lasted that long," Asher said.

Penn flipped him off.

I laughed and stepped through the door and onto the plane. My heart was racing like crazy. A lot of it was the burning desire to get the fuck out of the country, but a good percentage of it was because, even with nasty words, the banter with Penn made me wet as hell.

We made our way to the back of the plane. I felt like I was getting on the bus to go to high school. Of course then I always sat at the front. But I wished I was one of those kids who dared to sit at the back and get up to whatever they did back there. Not that I necessarily wanted to be bad, but the kids up the back seemed to have a freedom the rest of us didn't.

It was all an illusion, I know that now, but back then it seemed like they had all the fun.

Now it was me having all the fun. Me and my amazing, sexy guys.

Tully, Asher, Zeke and I sat in a row of four seats. Penn, Landon and Channing sat across the aisle from us. Jackson, Violet and her men sat directly in front. That arrangement worked perfectly when Zeke threw a blanket over us both and snuck his hand up my skirt.

Only if anyone came down the back of the plane to use the toilet would they suspect what was going on. Hopefully everyone went before they boarded the plane.

Zeke parted my thighs gently with his fingers

and teased my panties aside. He stroked his finger-tips over the front of my pussy before delving down lower to my clit and folds.

He leaned in to whisper, "You're so wet."

"You're so hard." I slipped my hand down onto his cock. He felt like a rock under his jeans.

"Need some help there?" Asher asked from the other side of Zeke. He slipped his hands under the blanket and undid the front of Zeke's pants.

"I could use some help." Zeke lifted his hips to help pull them down far enough to free his erection.

While Asher traced circles around his tip with his fingers, I worked mine down lower to massage his balls. At the same time, I tucked up my knee so Zeke could slip his fingers inside me.

On the other side of me, Tully palmed my nipples through the fabric of my shirt, and guided my other hand to his already bare cock which was hidden by another blanket.

It wasn't easy, but I managed to coordinate my movements so my hands were sliding up and down both guys at the same time. Judging by the way the blanket in front of Asher rose and fell, Zeke was doing the same to him.

We all fell still and looked as innocent as we could as an attendant checked on us and made sure the overhead baggage lockers were all closed, ready for takeoff.

Something was ready for takeoff all right. Several somethings. All of them hot and hungry.

The attendant, not the one who flirted with the guys, gave us all a look like she knew we were up to something, but moved on. She probably saw a million crazy things while on the job. This might be tame in comparison. At least we weren't going to get drunk and violent.

Drunk maybe. Violent no. At least, I hoped not.

She moved back to the front of the plane as the aircraft started to taxi towards the runway.

"Almost made it," Asher said.

"That was quick," Zeke said teasingly. "I know I have mad skills, but I didn't realise I was that good."

Asher laughed, low and husky with desire. "Yes you do, and you are, but I'm not that quick. I'll leave that to Penn."

"Fuck off," Penn said from the other side of the plane. Apparently he was listening in to the conversation.

I glanced over to see him with a blanket over his lap. Evidently he was doing more than just listening. Remembering him watching us the other night made me even hotter. I was one lucky girl.

Asher might not be that quick, but I was. It only took a dozen or two strokes of Zeke's fingers on my G spot, while the heel of his hand rubbed my clit, and Tully rolling my nipples between his thumb and finger, for me to come.

I bit my lip to keep from screaming, because that might have resulted in the plane being turned around and us being kicked off.

We hadn't come this far to have me risk us by having an orgasm. That would definitely be the worst orgasm ever.

Even after I came, Zeke and Tully kept working me until the pressure started to build again.

Underneath me, the plane rumbled and started to pick up speed. As it did, my hand picked up speed as well. Both guys rolled their hips and thrust into my fingers, their breathing quiet but ragged.

I couldn't help feeling powerful and sexy with both of their cocks in my hands. I enjoyed making them feel good and the fact they all wanted me was even hotter. A girl could certainly get used to this. Maybe with a king-size bed next time.

Although, we were making do pretty well.

The engine roared. The front wheels of the plane lifted off the ground. A second later, the back wheels followed.

A second after that, I came again at the same time Zeke and Tully came in my hands. My stomach dropped with the momentum of the plane at the same time my orgasm rose. It was a strange sensation, but not unpleasant. It was heightened by the feeling of warm, pearly cum on my fingers.

Asher was only a couple of moments behind the other guys, just as the sound of the wheels tucking up into the plane echoed through the cabin.

"We fucking made it," Zeke said with relief.

"We made it fucking," Tully said with a grin.

We all laughed and sagged together under our blankets. All I wanted to do now was curl up and sleep until we arrived in Singapore.

And hope like fuck the trouble didn't follow us all the way there.

ABBIE

"I NEVER THOUGHT I'd be glad to be away from Australia," I said.

Our suitcases even made it all the way here with us.

Bonus.

Maybe things would start to turn around from now on. We could all use a bit of good luck and relaxation for a change. And by relax, I mean focus on the tour.

There was nothing relaxing about it, really, but we all loved performing, so it never felt like a chore. Well, unless people were throwing cans at us.

"Same here." Tully slipped his hand into mine as we walked through Changi airport.

This must be the cleanest airport in the world. It

was certainly right up there at the top. I felt dirty walking through it, like I should have washed before I came somewhere so clean and tidy.

Thank fuck it wasn't too far to the hotel where I could have a shower.

"I know we shouldn't rest completely, but I feel like I can breathe now," Asher said.

"At least until the next flight," Zeke said. He nodded towards a board which showed the next ten or fifteen flights which would land. It didn't show another one from Perth, but it wouldn't be long. No one doubted Hunter and Parker would be on board.

"I'm starting to feel like we're on that show where they travel around the world and teams race each other," Landon said. "We got on the first flight out of Perth, but sooner or later they'll catch up with us at some kind of challenge. With any luck, it'll be a singing or dancing one, not eating gross food." He made a face in disgust.

"I wish that was all it was," Tully said. He looked tired, and his usual smile and good humour were nowhere to be seen.

Killing your father was something anyone would take time to bounce back from. Even though they weren't related by blood, I knew Tully loved the man. Things must have been extreme for him to do what he did.

So far, he hadn't gone into much detail. I hoped at some point he would open up to me about what really happened.

"We all do," Zeke said. "Let's pretend for a while we're just rock stars on a world tour."

"I can pretend that," Asher said.

"Of course you can," Penn said. "You've been pretending to be a rock star for years."

Asher turned and stuck his tongue out at Penn. "You're just jealous of my good looks."

Penn snorted.

"I'm sorry to interrupt your charming conversation," I said, "but I need to use the ladies room."

They all hesitated.

"I can go in by myself," I told them. "I'll only be two or three minutes. Promise."

Zeke reluctantly nodded. "We'll be right outside. If you need anything, just shout."

"Anything at all." Asher grinned.

I patted the drummer on the cheek and slipped into the women's toilet. As tempting as his offer was, I felt messy. I wanted to shower before I got intimate with any of them again.

I hurried past the basins and into the area that held the cubicles.

I didn't pay much attention to anyone else who was in there with me, I just locked the door behind me and did what I needed to do.

As I reached to undo the latch, heavy footsteps stopped outside the door.

My first instinct was to freeze. I reminded myself the guys were outside. Close enough to hear me if I screamed for help. Assuming I could actually do that in time.

The footsteps paused for maybe half a minute, then walked on.

You're just being paranoid, I told myself. After everything that happened, a little bit of paranoia was understandable. Just because we got out of Perth, didn't mean everything was suddenly perfectly safe.

I decided to play it cool but keep my eyes and ears open. I stepped out of the cubicle and walked over to the sink to wash my hands.

I jumped as someone appeared behind me in the mirror.

"Abbie?"

I stared at his reflection, eyes wide.

What the fuck?

I knew the man who stood behind me. The

former owner of Onyx Riot Records and, very briefly, my lover.

"Pete? What the hell are you doing here?"

THANKS FOR READING! The story continues in book 4 Muse

Maggie Alabaster writes reverse harem and, paranormal, sci-fi and fantasy romance.

She lives in NSW, Australia with one spouse, two daughters, one dog, and countless birds.

Jo Bradley is her alternate personality. She writes contemporary romance.

Sign up for my newsletter! Sign Up!

Join my reader group! Join here!

Follow me on Bookbub! Click here to follow me!

Check out my website- www. maggiealabaster.com

ALSO BY MAGGIE ALABASTER

Dark Masque

Book 1 Bait

Book 2 Prey

Book 3 Trap

Saving Abbie

Book 1 Pitch

Book 2 Pound

Book 3 Session

Book 4 Muse

Book 5 Rhythm

Book 6 Encore

Ruthless Claws

Book 1 Ivory

Book 2 Crimson

Book 3 Elodie

Harmony's Magic

Book 1 Summoned by Fire

Book 2 Summoned by Fate

Book 3 Summoned by Desire

Shifter's Vault

Book 1 Discarded

Book 2 Deceived

Book 3 Disgraced

My Alien Mates

Book 1 Star Warriors

Book 2 Star Defenders

Book 3 Star Protectors

Academy of Modern Magic

Book 1 Digital Magic

Book 2 Virtual Magic

Book 3 Logical Magic

Complete Collection

Summer's Harem

Book 1: Shimmer

Book 2: Glimmer

Book 3: Flicker

Complete collection

Short reads

Taken by the Snowmen

Jingle All the Way

Also by Maggie Alabaster and Erin Yoshikawa

Caught by the Tide

Book 1–Pursued by Shadows

Book 2 Pursued by Darkness

Book 3 Pursued by Monsters